FLY LIKE THE SEAGULL

Stories By

Nathan Graziano

Luchador Press
Big Tuna, TX

Copyright © Nathan Graziano, 2020
First Edition 1 3 5 7 9 10 8 6 4 2
ISBN: 978-1-952411-05-2
LCCN: 2020935485

Cover image and design: Jacob Dandy
Author photo: Paige Graziano

Acknowledgements:

Some of these stories originally appeared in *The Trailer Park Quarterly*, *Mad Swirl* and *The Philosophical Idiot*.

"The Story of The Seagull" originally appeared, under a different title, in the book *Almost Christmas*, published by Redneck Press in 2017.

I'd like to acknowledge the various writers and musicians whose words and lyrics I'm using here—illegally, albeit: The Cult (Ian Astbury and Billy Duffy), Van Halen (Michael Anthony, Alex Van Halen, Eddie Van Halen and David Lee Roth), Bruce Springsteen, WB Yeats and Tennessee Williams. Here's a preemptive thanks for not suing me.

A special thanks to Dr. Daniel Crocker, who named this book before I started writing it; my colleague and friend Carrie Thompson for the watchful eye; and, of course, my wife Liz, for putting up with me and The Seagull all these years.

Table of Contents:

Book I

Book II

Book III

Book IV

This is for all the lonely people

*I'm dying for some action, I'm sick of sitting 'round here
trying to write this book*

-Bruce Springsteen
"Dancing in the Dark"

Bide your time, for success is near.

-A Fortune Cookie

Book I

The Story of The Seagull

It was a Tuesday afternoon and raining, a downpour that deposited a shallow, murky pond in the dirt parking lot outside the bar. Inside, Toby and I were splitting pitchers and trying to score a gram. *Fox News* was muted on the television behind the bar, a silence that soothed me as the ticker on the bottom of the screen scrolled through the headlines.

A guy with a bald dome and inky black hair pulled into a tight ponytail walked in and sat on the stool beside Toby. He ordered a draft from Cindy and stared straight into the mirror behind the top-shelf bottles.

"Caw, caw, caw!" Toby called like a bird.

Startled, the man snapped his head to the side and stared at Toby, hard and unblinking, and as soon as Cindy finished pouring his beer, the man took his mug and moved to an empty table in the back, beneath a lighted Budweiser sign.

"What's that all about?" I asked Toby, waiting for a text.

"That's Jimmy Lucas," Toby said. "I worked with him at *The Northboro Times* about ten years ago. He had more hair then and a weird obsession with Steven Seagal. The guy walked around the warehouse like he was on the set of *Hard to Kill*, doing spin kicks and striking karate poses."

I got a text from a dealer but he was picking up outside of Northboro and wouldn't be back for two hours. "What's with the bird call?" I asked.

"Jimmy got a vanity plate for his car and he wanted it to read SEAGAL. But the fucker couldn't spell his last name so the license plate ended up spelling SEAGUL. So when he'd come into work, we'd make bird calls and yell, 'It's the Seagull!' Jimmy got so fed up that he ended up quitting. I think he works at a supermarket now. In the seafood section. Can you believe that? The Seagull sells fish?"

"You couldn't write that."

"You tell me," Toby said. "You're the writer."

"Not lately," I said. "I can't seem to get started on my next book." Then my phone buzzed, and it was a different guy. Bingo. I turned to Toby. "I can grab a gram but I have to meet the dude at the Mobile station, two blocks away, and it's pouring out."

"I don't mind getting wet," said Toby.

"I'll drive you." Like a ninja, The Seagull approached from behind without us noticing.

"Jimmy, you're my hero," Toby said.

"Call me The Seagull."

"It's you," I said. "You're the one I'm going to write a book about."

"You always knew," said The Seagull, his keys dangling from his index finger. "This was meant to happen. Namaste, Nate."

"Namaste, Seagull."

The Seagull was right. I always knew it was him, and this *was* meant to happen.

Happily Ever After

I met her in the produce section of the supermarket. She wore a white bow in her hair and a white sundress with blue polka dots. We were both standing by the Idaho potatoes, singing along with a Kenny Loggins's song piping from the ceiling. She grabbed a potato and held it in front of my face. "Look," she said. "It's Donald Trump."

I grabbed a potato and held it in front of her face. "Look," I said. "Mike Pence."

We laughed for a few moments. Then we cried for a few more. I wiped her eyes with a handkerchief I didn't know I had in my pocket.

"Do you like avocados?" she asked.

"I adore avocados," I told her.

We spent the next three weeks finding the two ripest avocados, and I gave her the best one because chivalry isn't dead, only resting like a dead man. "Do you like sushi?" she asked.

"I adore sushi," I told her.

It took us another month to find the sushi chef, who had a bald dome and inky black pulled into a tight ponytail. I knew him right away.

"Why aren't you wearing a chef's hat?" I asked The Seagull.

"You know the answer, Nate," he said.

My fiancée—I asked her to marry me while we were discussing the best brand of soy sauce—ordered the California rolls. "I don't trust the spicy tuna," she said.

The Seagull rolled his eyes. "I don't have time to talk about the tuna," he said.

We spent the next month feeding each other California rolls with chopsticks The Seagull promised were carved from one of Mickey Mantle's bats. We poured the soy sauce in our palms, cupping them like we were drinking from a fresh stream.

"Do you like coconut water?" she asked.

"I adore coconut water," I told her. And we spent the next three months drinking coconut water. Then she told me she was pregnant.

"I'm going to be a father."

She burst into tears. "No," she said between sobs. "The baby belongs to The Seagull."

As I was about to reveal to her the things resting in the ghostly chambers of my broken heart, and tell her I planned to dedicate my book to her, The Seagull arrived on a motorized cart. My fiancée got on the back, and they drove off into the parking lot. I watched as billowy white wings sprouted from The Seagull's shoulder blades and he scooped my ex-fiancée into his arms, the cart crashing into the concrete. And they flew into a deep-orange sunset, happily ever after.

After several months of gaining weight and leveling out on Celexa and Seroquel, I began the mental preparation to write the book you're about to read—the one about The Seagull.

The Day I Went to See David Lee Roth

I read about the event in a free weekly that was delivered to my apartment, one of those local tabloids composed mostly of advertisements for tanning salons and burrito vans. I was balking at my book, needing to clear my head and get out of the apartment. When I first read about the article, I was incredulous. In no way did I believe David Lee Roth would come to Northboro. But it turned out to be true. He was doing a radio spot then a book signing for *Crazy from the Heat*, his memoir about those rockin' times on the road with Van Halen, when he wore parachute pants and did Teddy Bear jumps onstage, and slept with so many beautiful women that their beauty became an afterthought.

Yes, sir, Diamond Dave was coming to Northboro, and I was hell-bent on getting my copy of *Crazy from the Heat* signed.

I waited on the sidewalk outside of the radio station wearing black parachute pants and a shredded red tank top falling off my shoulder. I held the book to my chest while reciting the lyrics to "Yankee Rose" in spoken word.

But Diamond Dave must've taken the back way out of the studio. Someone must've tipped him off.

So I went to the bookstore and waited outside the café, in front of the Psychology section with a guy who had a bald dome and inky black hair pulled into a tight ponytail. The Seagull was drinking a latte.

"I didn't know you were a David Lee Roth fan," I said to The Seagull, still miffed that he stole my fiancée.

"I'm a huge David Lee Roth fan. I celebrate all things hedonistic. I am one debauched bird, Nate."

"Do you keep a drink in your hand and your toes in the sand?"

5

"Come on, Nate, give me a break."

"One break, coming up!"

The Seagull smiled. "How's the book coming?"

"How's my fiancée?"

"That snappy little mammy gonna keep her pappy happy and accompany me to the ends of the earth," said The Seagull.

"Well-played," I conceded.

The Seagull and I waited another forty-five minutes but the line never got any longer and David Lee Roth never showed up. Instead, we got Mexican food from a burrito van. I ordered the Grande Burrito, and The Seagull had the fish tacos.

When I got home, I sat down at my desk and I started to type.

Book II

Tinder Date

This Tinder-thing had Eloise scratching her hands raw, her eczema flaring the second she swiped right. She now stared into her daughter's closet, scratching, trying to decide on something to wear for her date. Alyssa, her only child, was sleeping at a friend's house for the night—or so Alyssa, a senior at Northboro High School, told her mother. Eloise, however, suspected she was staying with her boyfriend in his dorm room at Northboro College.

At forty-two, Eloise felt too old, too desperate, too un-hip to be using a dating application and wearing a teenager's dress. Who was she kidding? Tinder wasn't a dating app; it was a no-strings attached/come-over-and-fuck app. But Eloise mustered her courage and picked out a form-fitting strapless blue dress her daughter wore to the homecoming dance that fall. It fit Eloise perfectly, a small point of pride.

Meanwhile, Eloise's estranged spouse, Al, had been checking off the boxes in his textbook midlife crisis.

Twenty-two-year-old blonde girlfriend named Tiffany. Check. A sporty new convertible. Check. Hair transplants from Dr. Dick Doyle's Male Enhancement Clinic. Check. A gym membership and a year's supply of Creatine shakes. Check and another check.

A retired firefighter, Al moved out that summer, paid Eloise a year's worth of child support, and drove off with Tiffany—top down and transplanted pubic hair blowing in the breeze—to San Diego to work with his brother who had opened a marijuana dispensary.

"Fuck Al," Eloise muttered while changing into a clean bra and panties and squeezing back into the dress. She knew by the way the boys in her Intro to Literature classes at Northboro College sometimes stared at her— the muffled "MILF" comments that were easier to ignore—that she was attractive and desirable. Still, self-doubt loomed, and she used a picture from her mid-thirties for her Tinder profile, a picture that Al snapped on the deck of a Carnival Cruise of Eloise in a red bikini, and less than ten minutes after activating her account, she received her first request.

His name was Jimmy, and he lived on the outskirts of Northboro. From his profile picture, he looked a little like a young Steven Seagal with a prominent jaw and thick black hair pulled back into a tight ponytail. He didn't list a specific age, simply "in the middle of things," and included fishing, performance poetry and martial arts as his hobbies. He was attractive, and, quite frankly, Eloise wanted to get laid; she wanted something else to fill a cold pit inside her that brimmed with anger and shame and Chardonnay since Al left. So Eloise arranged for Jimmy to pick her up at her house, a decision that now seemed impetuous and foolish. Part of her, however, embraced the spark of danger as it lit that cold pit.

She walked downstairs and poured herself a glass of wine and sat at the kitchen table. She was the mother of a teenage girl, an adjunct college professor, a member of a book club consisting of insipid housewives who—many moons ago—were undergraduate English majors, but now they seldom talked about Virginia Wolf; instead, they used the book club meetings to complain about their husbands' limp dicks and their children's activities that peppered their already-busy schedules. Maybe Eloise was too old to be wasting her time on a frivolous fling, something she seldom did when she was single.

The doorbell rang, and Eloise downed the wine and applied a fresh layer of rose-colored lipstick.

She stood up in her daughter's slinky dress and made her way to the front door, taking long breaths. When she opened it, the man standing on the steps had a bald dome and inky black hair pulled into a tight ponytail. He vaguely resembled Steven Seagal, only the bloated and washed-out Steven Seagal living in Russia after his movie career crashed.

"You must be Jimmy," Eloise said, unable to conceal the disappointment in her voice.

"You can call me The Seagull," he said then leapt into the air and did a series of spin kicks. When he was finished, he pressed his palms together in front of his chest and bowed his head. "Namaste, Eloise," he said.

Eloise pressed her hands together and bowed. "Namaste, Seagull," she said and watched as The Seagull sprouted billowy white wings from his shoulder blades and flew toward a patch of purple clouds blanketing the late-evening sky.

Eloise smiled then went back into the house, poured another glass of wine and ordered Chinese food, having a hankering for the shrimp fried rice.

An Art Film at Fenway Park

Jocelyn wore a white bow in her hair, a detail Dennis symbolically placed in the screenplay. They were filming a piece he wrote for his Advanced Filmmaking class, a short film titled *A Seagull Shits on Her Head.* Aleister Bowman, Dennis's professor at Northboro College, loved the screenplay, calling it a "postmodern masterpiece" and "Albee-esque." Perpetually martini-bombed, Professor Bowman disappeared later that fall, running off with a theater student named Miguel. An adjunct named Allan Ginsburg replaced him. Of course, it wasn't the poet Allen Ginsberg—it's a different spelling, as you can see. As for Professor Bowman, the last anyone heard of him, he was directing *The Iceman Cometh* for the Northboro Community Players with Miguel cast as Hugo, the drunken Communist. But this was years ago, and Dennis no longer makes films or writes screenplays. With his undergraduate degree in Film Studies, he now works for his cousin's moving company during the day and drives an Uber at night.

This was a brisk autumn night in September, and the Red Sox were playing the Marlins at Fenway Park. Dennis and Jocelyn sat in The Green Monster seats above the historic thirty-seven foot left field wall. Their cameraman, Dennis' roommate Matt, scored the three tickets from the owner of the restaurant in downtown Northboro where he bused tables. Matt gave the owner— an oily Pakistani who wore thick gold jewelry pressed against tufts of thick black body hair—a handjob for the tickets. At the time, Matt denied his sexuality and, instead, labeled himself a patron of the arts. Recently, Matt married the love of his life in a beautiful summer wedding on Provincetown, and he and Ryan now own a house with a yellow-Lab named Allan Ginsburg.

But that's all backstory. Let's now delve into the narration and return to that Tuesday night at the ballpark.

The couple sitting next to Dennis and Jocelyn wore wigs. Grossly overweight with a graying walrus mustache, the man wore a black Cher wig with bangs as straight as a measured line, and his partner, a woman with an angular face and high cheek bones, donned a mullet wig and spoke with a slow, strained Slovakian accent. They held up a sign with black letters on a red poster board that read, *You're eating dolphin NOT tuna.*

The couple wasn't written into Dennis' screenplay but sometimes one must believe in serendipity. They were perfect for the film.

During The Seventh Inning Stretch, Jocelyn and Dennis appeared on the Jumbo-tron in centerfield. Dennis knew some people at the ballpark and pulled some strings, desperately wanting to impress Professor Bowman. While on the Jumbo-tron, he knelt in front of Jocelyn and held a red velvet box with an Ambien inside. "Will you sleep with me?" Dennis asked Jocelyn as Matt filmed.

The crowd believed that it was a legitimate marriage proposal—life and not art—and held their collective breath. The man in the Cher wig sang a dolphin love song in perfect pitch.

As scripted, Jocelyn, playing a non-binary named Jo, thumbed her nose at Dennis and walked away, leaving him abandoned, kneeling and alone—an artful tableau of a broken man holding an Ambien in a red velvet box.

"Great art always makes the audience uncomfortable," Professor Bowman once told the class before passing out at his desk.

But when the crowd jeered Jocelyn, Dennis knew the film was ruined. She was supposed to be the heroine.

The cameraman for the Jumbo-tron, sensing something amiss, pulled away and focused on a fat kid twerking to "Living on a Prayer" by Bon Jovi, his white belly jiggling above his beltline.

Ten minutes later, Jocelyn returned with two beers and a tray of nachos. "I forgot my next line," she said to Dennis.

"There is no next line," Dennis whined, holding his head. "It's all gone to hell. The movie is ruined."

Then a guy selling peanuts, a man with a bald dome and inky black hair pulled into a tight ponytail, stopped next to them. "Take the bow out of your hair," he said to Jocelyn.

"Who are you?" she asked, removing the bow.

"I'm The Seagull and I'm here to save the film."

Elated, Dennis asked, "Who gave you the screenplay, Seagull?"

On cue, the couple with the wigs stood and clapped slowly while they wept. The Seagull sprouted billowy white wings from his shoulder blades and flew toward the Citgo sign above Fenway Park, shitting on Jocelyn's bow-less head. Distracted by the fat kid twerking, Matt failed to capture the scene on film.

Strip Poker on Christmas Eve

It's seldom simple and never sequential, those moments when you slip into the second-person. You meet these two women at a bar on Christmas Eve, and they bring you back to their small second-floor apartment in a seedier section of Northboro. You're now sitting at a kitchen table with the women and a guy with a bald dome and inky black hair pulled into a tight ponytail, preparing to play strip poker at three a.m.—technically now Christmas Day. The women then break out the eggnog and brandy, and a generous pile of cocaine.

In the kitchen of this drab two-bedroom place, white Christmas lights are strung across the tops of the plywood cupboards, and there's a plastic candelabra on the counter next to four thick rails of blow. You indulge in a line—the coke is fine—and now you're grinding your teeth, noticing that the eggnog is sour and the brandy watered down. Both women are wearing cowboy hats and winter coats. The Seagull sports a simple white jumpsuit.

"Let's play straight poker. Fuck Texas Hold 'Em," says the thinner of the two women. She has a scar above her top lip and a slight lisp. "I used to live in Denton, and that whole state can suck my tit."

Her roommate, a redhead with haunting sky-blue eyes, shuffles the cards as she hums "Silent Night" and rubs her foot against your shin under the table. As *It's a Wonderful Life* plays on a muted television in the living room, you realize you've never been this alone.

"We should've gotten a Christmas tree," Blue Eyes says to Texas.

"Just deal," Texas says, wiping her nose with her sleeve. "We'll get naked and imagine a tree."

"That sounds divine," says Blues Eyes and winks at you. "I forgot your name."

"Call me Clarence," you say, convinced you're the guardian angel of someone, in a place where no bells ring and no one gets their wings.

"And you?" Blue Eyes looks at The Seagull.

"You know my name," he says. "You always knew."

"Deal the cards," Texas says. She's now in black and white and the most beautiful thing you've ever seen outside of color, her scar glowing like a streak of lightning above her lip.

Blue Eyes deals the cards and places her foot on your crotch. You look at your hand and grin. You and The Seagull stay. Blue Eyes takes three cards, and Texas—in black and white—takes one. Blue Eyes flips the turn.

The Seagull hoots. "Loosen your garments, girls," he says. "You too, Clarence." He throws down his cards. The Seagull has three queens. Blue Eyes and Texas—who is still in black-and-white—throw down their cards and take off their hats. Their hair is angelic, glowing red and gray, respectively. Texas' scar seems to hum.

They stare at you. You might be weeping as you show them your cards.

"I knew it," The Seagull says to you and takes off his jumpsuit. Billowy white wings sprout from his shoulder blades. "Thank you, Clarence," he says and opens the kitchen window and flies into the night, church bells ringing.

Rain on the Parade

Adam's fourteen year-old daughter Kayla hadn't lifted her head from her phone since he picked her up at his ex-wife Sarah's apartment. Head down, she fired off texts to her friends at a frenetic pace, her thumbs tap-dancing on the screen. On the ride to the St. Patrick's Day parade in downtown Northboro, Adam tried to engage his daughter in some light banter but her responses were either monosyllabic or short grunts of recognition.

At the parade, they stood on the sidewalk next an elderly couple wearing dark sunglasses and drinking large mugs of milk through straws. Ominous clouds swirled overhead, threatening rain or sleet or frogs. The Northboro High School band marched past, playing The Cult's "Sweet Soul Sister" from the band's epic 1989 album *Sonic Temple*—the song was, coincidentally, Adam and Sarah's wedding song.

"Your mom and I had our first dance as a married couple to this song," Adam said, remembering Sarah on their wedding day, stunning in her white satin gown.

Kayla grunted without lifting her head.

Behind the marching band, Northboro's mayor, Gerry Lafleur—a corpulent old French-Canadian with broken capillaries blotching his nose and cheeks—sat on the hood of a blue Ford Pinto, waving like a beauty pageant queen. The mayor's son Todd was now dating Sarah so Adam despised the mayor through proxy.

The elderly couple waved back to Mayor Lafleur.

"If it weren't for the fact that he emptied the senior centers, bribing them with free milk and busing them to the polls, he never would've been voted into office," Adam said, nudging Kayla.

"Right," she said.

The elderly man, sipping his milk, stuck out his ass and farted in Adam's direction.

Next, Miss Northboro rode a burro in a red sequined dress and a sash, giving the double-thumbs up to the crowd like a politician. She reminded Adam of a young Sarah.

"Does your mother still cry when it rains?" Adam asked his daughter.

She grunted, not looking up, not even after the burro stopped, brayed and shat in the center of the road. The elderly man ran out and wafted the fumes in Adam's direction.

As soon as the burro's mess was removed from the parade route, a float meant to resemble the rolling green hills of Ireland came barreling down Main Street. The float was covered in lime-colored Astroturf with a papier-mâché rainbow and a black plastic pot filled with golden plastic chips. A man with a bald dome and inky black hair pulled into a tight ponytail was standing beside the pot, dressed as a leprechaun in a green topcoat and knickers.

"Top of the mornin'," The Seagull said in a strained Irish brogue and bowed. He then spotted Adam and Kayla and stared at them.

What happened next can only be confirmed by Adam and the elderly couple. In fact, his fidelity to the truth of this account will land Adam in The Clear Waters Center, a mental health facility in downtown Northboro, where he'll be admitted for a second time later in this book. The rest of the parade-goers claim no such things ever happened.

And Kayla, of course, was staring at her phone.

In Adam's recollection, however, the float came screeching to a halt in the middle of the road. "What is happening?" Adam asked.

Head down, Kayla shrugged and grunted and shrugged.

"*Time hustles those who wait to die,*" The Seagull sang in a perfect Ian Astbury voice.

The elderly man dropped his milk, shattering the mug. "That's no leprechaun. That's The Seagull," he said.

The green topcoat split down the back and billowy white wings sprouted from The Seagull's shoulder blades. He picked up a megaphone. "Get off your phone," he called to Kayla.

He then flew over the papier-mâché rainbow and into the dark clouds that spit raindrops then The Seagull disappeared.

Finally, Kayla looked up. "What did I miss?" she asked.

Adam placed a hand lightly on his daughter's shoulder. "Everything, love. You missed everything."

Open Mic Night at The Java Café

L ewis arrives early at The Java Café so he can secure a table in close proximity to the open-mic sign-up list, manned by the poet James C. Hoffman, host of *The Northboro Gathering of Words*. The list opens at 6 p.m. sharp, and the reading begins promptly at 6:30 p.m. Lewis, a substitute teacher at Northboro High School, has been attending the open-mic nights for three months, since his wife Lydia moved out of their house and took up with Andre Whittaker, the piano player for The Andre Whittaker Jazz Trio— who play Dave Brubeck covers on Thursday nights at La Carreta's, a Mexican restaurant in downtown Northboro. Lewis has been writing poems since taking a creative writing class with Professor Aleister Bowman at Northboro College twelve years ago, jotting down his verse in a cork-covered notebook with a quill pen he purchased online whenever the muse arrives. But he has been reluctant to share his poems since the horrible incident with Lydia.

One night, after they both had multiple margaritas at La Carreta's—taking in the dulcet sounds of the Andre Whittaker Trio—Lewis shared a few of his lighter pieces with his wife. Upon reading Lewis' poems, Lydia shot him a look like he'd grown a beak. A month later, she was moving out of their house and into Andre Whittaker's townhouse on the outskirts of Northboro.

Meanwhile, the poet James C. Hoffman is sitting with his paramour Wendy Devoe at the sign-up table in the back of the café. As the wall clock strikes 6 p.m., he clears his throat and strokes his graying beard. "The open-mic sign-up list is now…open," he says and hands Wendy Devoe a pen like he is presenting her with Excalibur.

Wendy Devoe has been an insufferable snob since having a poem accepted in *The Northboro Review*, the college's literary journal. It's a detail she never fails to mention every time she reads the poem. With her bifocals resting low on the bridge of her long sloping nose, she reads the poem in a sing-song poet-voice that sounds a like a kindergarten teacher reading a story about kittens to her class.

Beside the sign-up list, the poet James C. Harrison keeps a stack of his self-published chapbook, *Amalgamations of the Abstract Mind*, and for mere ten dollars, he'll sell you a chapbook and sign it for you, too.

Lewis stands in the back of a small line of poets signing up to read, which includes a hipster college student in skinny jeans with a man-bun, a frumpy older woman named Gail who reads mostly long odes to serial killers—her ode last month to Aileen Wuornos was undoubtedly her most graphic—and a new guy with a bald dome and inky black hair pulled into a tight ponytail. When it is finally his turn to sign up, Lewis takes the pen and looks at the sheet for the available slots.

"Are you reading tonight, Lewis?" the poet James C. Harrison asks him.

Lewis holds his cork-covered notebook tightly against his chest. "Tonight, I'm alive," he says.

"I'm looking forward to finally hearing you," the poet James C. Harrison says and smiles.

"Isn't that exciting," says Wendy Devoe, the competitive bitch.

The reading begins at exactly 6:30 p.m. The poet James C. Harrison welcomes a crowd of approximately a dozen people as an espresso machine roars in the background. There's a wooden podium in front of a picture window looking out on Main Street. The poet James C. Harrison begins by reading a poem from his chapbook—available for sale at his table for ten dollars—then gives the podium over to that haughty wench Wendy Devoe.

Wendy Devoe stands behind the podium and theatrically scans the crowd as a small smile, as thin as a scribble, breaks from her lips. She takes a deep breath and shuffles through the stack of papers she's holding. "This first poem was accepted for publication in *The Northboro Review*," she says and pauses so the crowd can take in her glory. "This is called 'Fishing with My Grandfather, Point Judith, 1981'."

Wendy Devoe, the pretentious whore, reads for fifteen minutes, although the allotted time is limited to five, and when she finishes, she takes off her bifocals, allowing them to dangle from the beaded glasses chain around her neck. She then presses her hands together and bows her head. "Namaste," she says to the audience and walks back to the table to a smattering of applause.

The poet James C. Harrison steps back to the podium. "Thank you, Wendy. As always, your work is inspiring, transformative, thought-provoking and sublime," he says. "Our next poet is a new to *The Northboro Gathering of Words*. Please welcome The Seagull."

From the restroom in the back, The Seagull runs full speed to the podium. He is now wearing a floral meal-sack dress and a gray wig with a bun in the back, his inky black ponytail poking out like a rat's tail. He then stands into front of the microphone, breathing-heavy and carrying a paper bag. He places the bag on the ground and holds up an index finger while catching his breath. "This is called 'Outtakes from *Psycho*'," The Seagull says.

He reaches into the bag and places three items on the podium: a rubber butcher's knife, a plastic bottle of ketchup and a white shower curtain. He then shakes out the curtain and holds it in front of him before abruptly dropping it and loosing an ear-piercing scream. He takes the rubber knife and stabs at the air, drops the knife and grabs the ketchup bottle and squirts ketchup all over his chest and torso. He then runs out of The Jarva Café, leaving the crowd stunned.

Seconds later, the poet James C. Harrison points out the picture window. "Look!"

Everyone in the audience huddles around the window. Again, Lewis is clutching his cork covered notebook to his chest, knowing it won't be opened. Not tonight. No one can follow this performance.

They watch as The Seagull sprouts billowy white wings from his shoulder blades and flies into the night sky, silhouetted by the moon.

And Wendy Devoe, that beautiful soul, weeps into her hands.

The Story of The Pelican

It was 1993, Tony's junior year at Northboro High School, and he was standing beside his locker, summoning the courage to cross the hallway and ask Allison Dunn to the junior prom. He took a deep breath, willing his feet to move. While asking a girl to a dance can produce some low-grade anxiety in the most cocksure teenage Romeo, Tony's anxiety was exacerbated by what he considered a deformity, a deal-breaker with the ladies: his prodigious honker.

Tony had inherited his mother's prominent nose, long and hooked with a bump on the bridge. It wouldn't have been as bad if he hadn't inherited his father's tiny, squinty eyes and small puckered mouth. As with many things in life, proportion was the problem. At night, after completing his homework—Tony was a stellar student—he would lie in his dark bedroom, imagining a new face, making his nose a diminutive button above his top lip, in perfect proportion with his other features. But eventually he'd wake up with the real Tony, whose hands were sweating as he treaded in a sea of teenage insecurity.

Allison stood alone, unprotected by her herd of girlfriends. Tony sat behind her in Mr. Luccadamo's geometry class, and while most girls ignored Tony, largely due to his reticence, Allison talked to him with a good-natured ease and laughed with her soft girlish giggle at Tony's wry jokes.

He finally wiped his hands on his Pearl Jam t-shirt and resolved, once again, to make his move. Then he went for it. He made it safely across the hallway and was standing behind Allison, close enough to smell her strawberry-scented shampoo. His mouth was parched, his legs shaking as he tried to tap her bird-like shoulder before he was bumped into Allison from behind. Allison gasped and spun around, facing Tony with her lips in a tight scowl.

"Watch where you're going, Pelican," Matt Rogers's voice rang out behind him. Matt and his toadies—Darren Walters and Todd LaFleur—stood there, hawing and elbowing each other. Blood rushed to Tony's face, a full blush, and the bones of his nose vibrated like a tuning fork.

"I'm fucking with you, Pelican," Matt Rogers said with a soft punch to Tony's bony chest. Tony had known the three boys since elementary school when Matt coined the moniker during a science unit on birds in Ms. Brown's fifth grade class. "What are doing on this side of the hall? Are you sweet on Miss Allison?"

Allison rolled her eyes at Matt and placed her hand softly on Tony's shoulder, a comforting gesture. "Grow up, asshole," she said and walked away, disappearing down the hall.

Tony knew his moment had passed and shrunk into nothing more than a honking nose amongst smaller noses. He hung his head, biting his bottom lip and fighting back the pressure building behind his eyes.

"Are you hot for Allison Dunn, Pelican? Do you want to poke her with that big beak of yours? Do you want her to make sweet love to your snot-locker?"

Tony turned from the boys so they wouldn't see him cry. Meanwhile, a janitor with a bald dome and inky black hair pulled into a tight ponytail, pushing a mop and a bucket, came barreling down the hallway. The name sewn to the left breast of his shirt read *The Seagull*.

"Coming through," The Seagull yelled, heading straight toward Matt Rogers. Before Matt could move out of the way, The Seagull plowed into him, hitting Matt in the nose with the end of the mop. Blood gushed from Matt's nose as he fell to the floor, writhing and screaming.

The Seagull glanced over his shoulder, winked at Tony then disappeared down the hall as well.

When Tony tells this story to his wife now, he swears he saw billowy white wings sprout from The Seagull's shoulder blades, and Allison believes him. Why wouldn't she?

A Day at the Beach

In a cloudless sky, the sun beat down on Seth's balding scalp. His wife Melanie, a fastidious packer, had everything a young family could fathom for a day at the beach: towels and beach chairs, peanut butter and jelly sandwiches wrapped in aluminum foil, apple juice boxes, sunblock SPF-50, two red plastic pails and shovels, a first-aid kit and a bar of soap to scrub off the sand in the public shower before getting into the SUV for the ride back to suburban Northboro. Melanie packed everything, except for Seth's Yankee hat to protect his dome from the scorching summer sun.

He watched his wife apply a third coating of sunblock to Cody and Ella, who were jamming sand into their red plastic pails. Melanie wore a black one-piece bathing suit, claiming she had lost her bikini body after giving birth to Cody. Seth disagreed. In fact, her breasts were fuller now, her hips more voluptuous than when they met their freshman year at Northboro College, almost fifteen years ago.

Seth's phone buzzed, and he squinted behind his sunglasses as he read the message: *Home alone, imagining you inside me.*

Rubbing more sunblock on their kid's pale shoulders, Melanie looked at Seth and smiled, her own eyes hidden by large bug-like shades. While things had not been going well in their marriage, and their sex life had soured, Melanie still tried to connect with him. Seth knew she tried, and it compounded his guilt; he wished he had the guts to tell it to her straight. But he was, in fact, a Yankee fan. And when Seth looked back at her, he remembered Melanie sitting across from him in the television lounge of their dorm, and his pulse quickened, and he wished he never took up with that woman. But the compulsion to be close with his wife collided with his conscience, and his confessions remained on his cowardly Yankee-fan tongue as their kids played in the sand and the sun baked his bare head.

"Shark!" The thin woman's scream was shrill, a shiv to the temple.

On their blankets and towels and beach chairs, beneath umbrellas jammed into the sand, the beach crowd jumped to their feet, spilling their lukewarm Pepsi cans and iced coffees and Bud Lights jammed in beer koozies. The beachgoers straightened their spines and made visors with their hands, staring out at The Atlantic, looking for a dorsal fin.

"This was a test," the thin woman said, pulling at sides of wide straw hat. "We all need to remain vigilant."

Then everyone at the beach—aside from Seth and his family—filed into lines and formed a flash mob and danced to The Cult's "Sun King" piping through the small beach's intercom speakers. Then much to Seth's amazement, Melanie and Ella and Cody joined the flash mob, synchronized in their steps.

Seth's phone buzzed in his hand but he was too stunned to check it. The flash mob twerked, including a fat kid Seth recognized from a Red Sox game years ago. A man with a bald dome and inky black hair pulled into a tight ponytail strolled past him.

"You need to tell her," The Seagull said to Seth before snagging a half-eaten tuna sandwich from the hot sand and sprouting billowy white wings from his shoulder blades and gliding, effortlessly, through the clear blue sky toward an island, a thin black line on the ocean's horizon.

But not before shitting on Seth's red scalp.

Corn Dogs

Jed told Willy he'd buy him a corn dog at the Northboro County Fair if Willy stayed to watch the oxen pull. Jed had trained a team of oxen with Gail, the vice-president of his 4-H Club, and he wanted his best friend for moral support. However, if Willy pulled a no-show then Jed threatened to proceed with the necessary paperwork to terminate their friendship. Gail was a notary public so Willy knew Jed's threat had teeth, and Willy figured he'd better go.

Willy arrived at the fair wearing a yellow raincoat over a pair of boxer shorts, per Jed's request, and met up with Jed after the demolition derby. September—which is about to be personified because I'm tired and trying to be literary—had announced the arrival of autumn, blowing its cool breath against the back of Willy's bare neck. This, Willy knew, was an ideal time for a corn dog with a dollop of ketchup.

Jed and Willy approached the food van. The guy working had a bald dome and inky black hair pulled into a tight ponytail. He wore a white apron splattered with grease and food stains. Beneath the apron, The Seagull sported a faded black Michael Bolton t-shirt that read *Time, Love & Tenderness* on the front and listed Bolton's tour dates on the back.

"I didn't know you worked here, Seagull," Jed said.

"I don't usually," The Seagull said. "Nate put me here to liven things up. The premise was pretty dull."

"It worked," said Seth. "He has my interest."

The Seagull struck a karate stance then folded his hands on his chest and bowed. "Namaste, Seth," he said and turned to Jed. "I suppose you're going to want a corn dog."

"You must be clairvoyant," said Jed. "But I'm going to need three. I promised Willy a corn dog if he stayed for the oxen pull. And grab Nate one, too. He's tired and hungry. Did you see that shitty personification of September he just wrote?"

"I threw up in my mouth," said The Seagull.

Standing behind Seth, Willy started running in place, working off the corn dog calories before they were consumed. Now trim and fit, Willy was a chubby kid, which made him a bit of an exercise junkie as an adult. I, on the other hand, though grateful for Jed's offer, declined the corndog, concentrating instead on my book.

"Don't pump your arms so much while running in place," The Seagull said to Willy, pulling two corn dogs from a fryolater.

"Thanks for the advice," Willy said, straightening his back, slowing down his arms as Jed took his corn dog and left to meet up with Gail and the oxen team and give them pre-pull pep talk .

"That's my job," The Seagull said and handed Willy his corn dog on a thin wooden stick. "There's one more thing." The Seagull summoned Willy forward with his index finger, leaning out of the truck and placing his mouth close to his ear. "You need to convince Jed to throw the oxen pull," The Seagull whispered. "I bet on the other team."

"You know I can't do that, Seagull," Willy said. "Nate won't let me."

"Then give me your raincoat," The Seagull said.

And Willy did. And then he was wearing only his boxer shorts, holding his corn dog. It started to rain, and The Seagull invited Willy inside the van and dropped some battered fish into the fryolator for them to share later.

Homecoming Game

Jason is attending the homecoming football game for the Northboro High School Seahawks, although he has no recollection of ever living in Northboro; yet once his ex-wife Amanda showed him a picture of a couple who looked like them in the 1993 NHS yearbook—they were voted "Class Sweethearts"—and Jason had to concede the concept was plausible.

Regardless, Jason loves homecoming games, no matter the location, and today he's sitting at the top of the metal bleachers next a man with a bald dome and inky black hair pulled into a tight ponytail who wears an old Northboro High School letterman jacket. The Seagull is holding a bag of popcorn and after each offensive down, he screams, "That's a helluva play, boys! Helluva play!"

Cloudless and crisp, the afternoon seems stolen from a postcard of The Big Sky in Montana, only Northboro is thousands of miles from Montana and a bit of a dilapidated hell-hole. Tad, the lithe and lean and agile quarterback for the Seahawks, throws a tight spiral sixty yards for his fourth touchdown pass in the first half. "Helluva of a pass, Tad," The Seagull yells through cupped hands. "Helluva pass!"

"This kid is an unearthly talent," Jason says.

"You got that right," The Seagull says. "His mother is short-listed for a Mars trip in 2025. If someone backs out, she's going to Mars and never coming back." He pauses then screams, "Let's go Seahawks. *Caw, caw, caw.*"

"Was that a bird call?" Jason asks.

"You got that right," The Seagull says. "It rallies the team. It's like the wind at their backs. It's like that Patrick Swayze song."

"'She's Like the Wind'?"

"That's a helluva memory, Jason. Helluva memory."

A person in the opposing teams' bleachers blows an air horn as the Northboro cheerleaders moonwalk to the marching band playing The Cult's "Edie (Ciao Baby)". Then the band and cheerleaders stop and freeze, wondering if my references to the songs on The Cult's 1989 album *Sonic Temple* are too self-indulgent and esoteric. They're wondering if I should stop playing the same damn album, over and over, while writing this book. The thought then passes, and the game resumes.

"What's the quarterback's last name?" Jason asks The Seagull.

"It's not pronounceable on this planet, only on Mars," The Seagull says. "Would you like some popcorn?"

"I quit," says Jason. "I haven't touched a kernel in nine months."

"That's over a year on Mars," The Seagull says and extends his hand. "Do you know my name?"

"I forgot it."

"You've always known, Jason."

With no earthly explanation, a deer runs across the fifty-yard line, and a hunter standing at the top of the visitors' bleachers shoots it dead. The cheerleaders scream and hug, turning from the carnage and consoling one another.

"Earth is a very dangerous place," says The Seagull. "I'm glad I don't live here."

The Seagull stands, dumps his popcorn and sprouts billowy white wings from his shoulder blades that rip through the back of his letterman jacket. "Let's go Hawks," he yells.

"Goodbye, Seagull," Jason says.

And without fanfare, The Seagull then flies into the cloudless sky as Tad throws his fifth touchdown pass, and Jason remembers pinning a corsage on a blue dress.

Fish Sticks

Thomas sensed imminent disaster this morning the second he set foot in Northboro High School's front lobby, a shrine celebrating seventy years of athletic dominance and academic apathy. Large glass cases contain tarnished trophies with faceless plastic athletes on the tops in sundry athletic poses—quarterbacks set to throw, point guards mid-jump shot—and plaques with effaced dates and the names of people long dead.

It is Thomas' first day at his new school in his new town—his parents split a month ago, sold their house in an affluent neighborhood in Middletown, and the only affordable apartment his mother could find for Thomas and his sister was in Northboro. And the moment he woke up in his new bedroom that morning, Thomas knew a disaster would be imminent and it would occur in the cafeteria, a notorious hunting ground for bullies. This is not to say that Thomas possesses paranormal powers. In fact, while slightly above-average in intelligence—and certainly not the genius he fancies himself—Thomas can be accurately described as dull. He doesn't participate in any activities or have any real interests, aside from video games, and the closest he's come to a date is humping his mattress after lifting a *Playboy* from a stash his father left behind in the garage.

Listen, I'm not trying to solicit pity for the kid. In fact, you'll likely feel differently when you read the story—some pages away—and he tries to reinvent himself as a pretentious twit and changes his name to Tomas, thinking it sounds more literary.

But, for now, we're in the cafeteria at ten minutes to noon with an imminent disaster staring down Thomas. In the front of the cafeteria, a line of students wait at the door to the kitchen, and at the exit, an old toad-like woman wearing a red visor sits on a wooden stool in front of a cash register. Thomas considers not eating lunch, taking a seat at one of the empty tables and pretending to read a book; however, he is starving and his mother, who forgot to pack his lunch this morning, gave him lunch money instead. Against his better judgment, Thomas ignores his premonition and waits in the back of the lunch line.

In front of him, three boys are laughing and pushing each other. The tallest of the three, the pack leader, pushes a squat kid into Thomas, knocking Thomas backwards on his ass.

As he falls, Thomas' glasses are knocked crooked on his face, and he looks up at the three boys, his eyes wide, then the look melts into something bashful and embarrassed, like he passed wind in an elevator. The low rumble in his gut tells Thomas this is the beginning of the imminent disaster he sensed several hours ago, and soon it will no longer be imminent. Just a disaster.

"Look what you did, Darren," says the tall kid holding out his hand to help Thomas to his feet.

"You're right, Matt. And I didn't properly apologize," says Darren, the squat kid with a pinched face. "Please accept my sincerest apologies."

Inside the kitchen, a commotion erupts. "The last time we had fish sticks they gave me six," a boy shouts. "Attica! Attica!"

The students in the lunch line are not interested in the threat of a riot; rather, they're watching Thomas and the three boys, hoping to see some good old-fashioned bullying.

Matt Rogers places his hand on Thomas' shoulder. "I noticed that you're new to the school. Do you have a name, old chap?"

Thomas stares down, avoiding eye contact.

"Thomas," he says under his breath.

"Good to meet you, T-Bone," Matt says. "These are my associates, Darren—whom you've met—and Todd, but his friends call him Todd. Now, T-Bone, do you have any idea what this fine establishment is known for, other than our sterling sports' programs?"

Darren and Todd move from Matt's flanks and stand behind Thomas.

"The answer, old chap, is The Northboro Atomic Wedgy," Matt says. "Gentlemen."

The next thing Thomas knows, Matt's goons strike from behind, each grabbing the waistband on Thomas's briefs, and they lift Thomas off the ground as the fabric of his underwear digs into his crotch. When it finally rips, Thomas is released. The crowd showers the boys with applause. Someone throws a rose at Matt Rogers, and he picks it up, places it between his teeth.

By the time the teachers on lunch duty make it there, after putting a stop to the fish stick insurgency, the crowd has dispersed and everyone proceeds as if nothing happened and no disaster occurred. Red-faced, Thomas scrapes his briefs from his crotch. He moves into the kitchen and grabs a tray, stopping in front of hotel pan full of fish sticks. The guy passing them out wears a hairnet, but beneath it he has a bald dome and inky black hair pulled into a tight ponytail. Thomas raises his tray, and The Seagull places six fish sticks on it.

"I thought we only got five," Thomas says.

The Seagull places an index finger to his lips. "Sometimes we all need an extra fish stick, Thomas."

There's a Blizzard Mid-book

All work and no play makes Nate a dull boy. All work and no play makes Nate a dull boy. All work and no play makes Nate a dull boy. All work and no play makes Nate a dull boy, all work and no play makes Nate a dull boy all work and no play makes Nate a dull boy, all work and no play makes Nate a dull boy. All work and no play, makes Nate a dull boy. All work and no play makes Nate a dull boy.

All work. And no play makes Nate a dull boy. All work and no play makes Nate a dull boy. All work and no play makes Nate a dull boy, all work and no play makes Nate a dull boy. All work and no play makes Nate a dull boy all work and no play makes Nate a dull boy all work, and no play makes Nate a dull boy. All work and no play makes Nate a dull boy; all work and no play makes Nate a dull boy. All work and no play makes Nate a dull boy all work and no play, makes Nate a dull boy.

All work and no play makes Nate a dull boy.

All work and no play makes Nate a dull boy, all work. And no play makes Nate a dull boy. All work and no play makes Nate a dull boy all work and no play makes Nate a dull boy all work, and no play, makes Nate a dull boy. All work and no play makes Nate a dull boy. All work and no play makes Nate a dull boy, all work and no play makes Nate a dull boy. All work and no play makes Nate a dull boy. All work and no play makes Nate a dull boy. All work and no play makes Nate a dull boy, no work and no play makes Nate a dull boy. All work and no play makes Nate a dull boy. All work and no play makes Nate a dull boy. All work and no play makes Nate a dull boy. All work and no play makes Nate a dull boy. All work and no play makes Nate a dull boy. All work and no play makes Nate a dull boy. All work and no play makes Nate a dull boy.

The Sword, the Selfie

Sean was crouched behind the bushes in front of his sister-in-law's apartment, holding a Samurai sword and waiting for his estranged wife Rochelle to arrive home from her date. Wearing black jeans and a black tank top, his chest and arms and shoulders sculpted and bulging, Hulk-like, Sean was ready to attack.

Earlier in the day, he worked his biceps and back for two hours at the gym, snapping selfies in the mirrors—nine, to be exact—with the blood pumping through his veins, his muscles stretching the fabric of his tank top. Sean forwarded the pictures to Rochelle, believing no woman could resist a man so jacked and soaked in masculinity. But Rochelle did not respond to any of the nine pictures, and Sean's friend Oliver—who Sean paid to spy on Rochelle—saw her earlier that morning at The Java Café having coffee with a local performance poet. Sean had banked on the nine muscle-bound selfies winning back his wife, who he lost after a brief and ill-advised fling with a stripper from The Dirty Bird, a club in a seedy section of downtown Northboro. When Rochelle found them naked together in the bedroom, Sean introduced the stripper as the new dog-walker for Prince Albert, their Great Dane.

Of course, Sean and Rochelle are fictional characters; although Sean is the real name of the guy I'm describing here, a guy who takes shirtless pictures of himself holding Samurai swords in various phallic poses, a veritable Freudian feast.

According to Rochelle, Sean also sends her pictures of his limp dick. Sean must believe that the juxtaposition of his pumped muscles and a flaccid penis—this is singularly my hypothesis—produces a dizzying effect on Rochelle, sending her into a sexual frenzy where she would chomp glass to get at Sean's sculpted frame and arouse that tentative cock.

Meanwhile, Sean waited in the bush with his Samurai sword for Rochelle and that poet fag to arrive at his sister-in-law's apartment where Rochelle was temporarily living. Was Sean contemplating impaling the nascent lovers? Was he going to jump from the bush and block their path, the black tank top discarded and the top button of his jeans undone, and challenge the poet to a pose down? Or would he simply scream, "Bonsai, motherfuckers!" and put a good scare in them?

Sean was weighing his options when he spotted two shadows splayed on the sidewalk, holding hands. He remained crouched and clasped the sword, ready to spring into action.

"I enjoyed dinner," a male voice said. "I like you, Rochelle."

"I like you, too, Seagull," she said.

Sean then jumped in front of Rochelle, his tall and beautiful blond wife, and a man with a bald dome and inky black hair pulled into a tight ponytail.

"Bonsai, motherfuckers," Sean screamed, swinging the Samurai sword at The Seagull.

The Seagull ducked and laid Sean out with a leaping roundhouse kick to the temple. He then took Rochelle's hand again as they stood over Sean's hulking, unconscious body.

"My hero," said Rochelle and kissed The Seagull softly on the lips.

"Namaste, baby."

Bereavement on Bennington Road

Priscilla, seventy-eight years old, took a third Xanax since her morning tea. Her primary care physician for fifty-six years, Dr. Richard Belmont—he went by "Richard," not "Dick," like her late-husband—prescribed her the light-blue football-shaped pills to treat her anxiety after Dick dropped dead from a thunderclap heart attack three weeks ago. Priscilla, however, didn't take a single pill after Dick stiffened with rigor mortis.

Truth be told, Priscilla hated Dick...

(Okay, now stop it. I know what you're thinking, but I'm not being sophomoric; the guy grew up in a generation of Dicks. He was eighty-four years old and grandfathered into the name. Everyone called him Dick, and not one eye was batted.)

Priscilla's problem with her husband, however, was not his name. It was the fact that Dick was a lifelong philanderer—something he adamantly denied when presented with a stranger's bra Priscilla found in the bedroom or lipstick on the collar of his shirt—and Dick was a mean drunk, spewing insults. She stayed with Dick while waiting for their forty-two-year-old agoraphobic son Donald, an only child, to get a job and move out of the house. But it never happened. Then Dick died. Priscilla discovered him limp on his Lay-Z-Boy in the den. While she went through the motions of grief, she quietly laughed into a tissue as dumb dead Dick was lowered into the ground.

Instead, it was the passing of her pet parakeet, Nugget, in proximity to her dipshit husband's death that made her hysterical with grief. Priscilla woke that morning, turned on the kettle for tea, and went to feed Nugget. There, she found the bird belly-up in its cage. For many years, while mired in a loveless marriage to

Dick, Nugget was her only companion. As her husband combed the breakfast restaurants for widows at the early-bird specials and Donald played his video games in his bedroom, Priscilla would drink tea and talk to Nugget, sometimes reading a chapter of a romance novel aloud to the bird.

After finding Nugget dead, Priscilla started sobbing inconsolably. She then dug the anxiety pills from a kitchen cupboard and popped a Xanax. An hour later, after her second cup of tea—Priscilla never drank more than three cups of Earl Grey in a day—she swallowed another one. Finally, she was relaxed enough to scoop Nugget's corpse from the cage and wrap it in a pink velvet handkerchief.

After she poured her third cup of tea and took the third Xanax, Donald walked into the kitchen, scratching his stomach. Donald was a tall man who wore his hair long and seldom changed out of his flannel pajama bottoms. He had a bevy of black t-shirts with sarcastic remarks printed on them. That day's t-shirt read, *My Alone Time Is for Your Safety*. Priscilla wondered if this shirt was worn without irony.

"What's that?" Donald asked, pointing at the handkerchief on the table, rolled like a spliff.

Priscilla would've cringed if her facial muscles hadn't been so relaxed. In fact, she paused before answering her son, taking a moment to acknowledge that the pills she took were pretty fucking fantastic. "Nugget passed away," she said. "He flew to a better place."

Donald shrugged and reached into the freezer, taking out a box of pizza-flavored *Hot Pockets*. "Can I have it?" he asked.

"Eat whatever you'd like," Priscilla said.

"I mean the bird's body," Donald said. "I might be able to sell it online."

Priscilla shook her head—the things her son said were almost as vile as the stuff that came out of Dick. "Donald, I'm grieving. Please respect that," she said as the doorbell rang. She and her son exchanged confused glances then Donald retreated to his room where he had a microwave.

Priscilla stood and floated from the kitchen chair to the front door. When she opened it, a man with a bald dome and inky black hair pulled into a tight ponytail stood on the front step holding a casserole dish.

"Can I help you?" Priscilla asked.

"I'm here to offer my condolences," The Seagull said and held out the casserole dish. "It's haddock."

"Who are you?" Priscilla asked.

"I'm a medium for birds," The Seagull told her. "Nugget said he misses you. Trust me. I know."

Priscilla wept as she took the casserole dish, mouthing the words "Thank you." But The Seagull was gone, sprouting billowy white wings from his shoulder blades and flying into a bright cloudless sky beside Nugget's ghostly image, both heading toward the heavens.

And there was not a Dick in sight.

'Til Death Do Them Part

Lauren had already crossed too many lines when she caught herself crossing the yellow lines on a dark road in the outskirts of Northboro, her car veering into the left lane before she pulled it back. She was smoking a cigarette with the window open, following the man driving the pick-up truck in front of her.

A part of her wanted to pump the brakes and head home before things progressed any further. Yes. She had kissed the man driving the pick-up truck in front of her, kissed him outside a bar while they shared a Winston Light. Yes. She was married and wearing her wedding ring when she met the man driving the pick-up truck in front of her. Yes. She had too many margaritas, three of which the man driving the pick-up truck in front of her bought. Yes. She was following the man driving the pick-up truck in front of her back to his place. Yes. Her husband Rocco was out of state on a business trip, and for the past six months, they had slept in separate rooms.

No. Lauren didn't feel good about her decision to follow the man driving the pick-up truck in front of her back to his place and pursue what she knew would amount to the final nail in her marriage's rickety wooden coffin.

Lauren was lighting another cigarette when her phone rang. She answered the call on speaker. "I'm driving and a little drunk," she said to her husband. "Is it an emergency?"

"I guess not. I just wanted to talk to you," Rocco slurred as Jimmy Buffet blared in the background above the hum of wet chatter in an Orlando bar. "I was thinking about you."

"I was thinking about you, too," Lauren lied. Well, it wasn't a complete fabrication. She was thinking about Rocco in an off-hand way, thinking about the consequences of what she was prepared to do with the man driving the pick-up truck in front of her. Would she fuck him, or would she stop at a oral sex? She caught herself, again, veering over the yellow lines and snapped the car back in her lane. "Do you want me to call you in the morning?"

"Where are you driving to?" Rocco asked.

Lauren paused, drew on her cigarette. "I'm driving home from a bar."

"I was thinking about you," her husband repeated.

"Good night, Rocco," Lauren said and ended the call, snubbing her half-finished cigarette out in the ashtray and flicking it out the window. She glanced at the floorboard beneath the passenger seat and spotted Rocco's Red Sox hat on the mat. Rocco wore that hat—battered and shabby, the brim broken into a permanent curve—anytime he was outside of work, and it surprised Lauren that he'd forgotten to bring it on his trip. When Lauren bought Rocco the hat for his thirtieth birthday, Rocco—a former third-baseman at Northboro College—took a baseball and bag of rubber bands then bent the brim of the hat around the baseball and secured it with the rubber bands. Lauren watched the process in awe, wondering why he was so concerned with the brim of his damn hat. They slept with the hat wedged between the box spring and the mattress for a week. Lauren was conscious of the small lump beneath her, and when he took it out, the brim was broken to her husband's liking.

The pick-up truck turned left into a community of townhouses, the moon a dumb yellow balloon in the night sky. She pulled beside the truck in a parking space. The man driving the pick-up truck stepped out and adjusted his cowboy hat, tipping the brim forward and hooking his thumbs inside a brass buckle shaped like an American eagle, and waited for Lauren to get out of her car.

"You sure are pretty," he said and kissed her on the cheek then lightly on her lips, then harder on her lips, slipping his tongue inside her mouth. "I'm the door on the left. I need to let the dog out, but you can make your pretty self comfortable," he said and went inside.

Lauren paused in the parking lot staring at the dumb moon balloon, remembering her husband's hat and grabbing it from her car as a guy with a bald dome and inky black hair pulled into a tight ponytail walked out from a neighboring townhouse

"Are you lost?" The Seagull asked Lauren.

She shrugged. "I'm not sure."

"You're lost," The Seagull said. Silhouetted in the porch light, billowy white wings sprouted from his shoulder blades. He was over to Lauren and scooped her into his arms and began flying toward the bulbous moon balloon.

"What is happening?" Lauren asked as they glided through the night sky.

"I'm saving your marriage," said The Seagull.

Now picture this: There's a full moon and in front of it, a giant bird-like man with a petite woman in his arms flies past. The woman is wearing a Red Sox hat with the brim perfectly broken in.

Book III

Bad Love on the Elliptical

Tiffany turned and watched Al on the elliptical machine beside her at Planet Fitness. She wondered all men sweat so profusely as they get older. Guys her own age—she was twenty-two—were gross in the ways all men are gross: they farted and scratched themselves and occasionally masturbated in her panties. But there was something particularly sad about watching a man get old, his hair disappearing from places it where belongs and reappears in stranger places—ears and nostrils, necks and nipples; there was something bilious and heartbreaking about watching a man talk to his dick before sex, like a coach giving a pep talk. Tiffany vaguely recalled a poem from her Introduction to Literature course at Northboro College where some guy was irked about getting old and sailed someplace where everyone got off on poetry or something. She remembered that the poem didn't make a lot of sense at the time and that Al's ex-wife—who taught the course—gave her a C-minus on a paper she wrote about it. The grade was a gift. Now she couldn't remember the name of the poem or the poet who wrote it.

While watching Al sweat, with his ear buds and hair plugs, his head nodding to whatever old-guy-electric-guitar music he was listening to—most likely The Cult's *Sonic Temple*—Tiffany decided it was time to follow through with what she'd been thinking about doing for weeks, since they returned from his midlife crisis road trip to California where Al was supposed to work at his brother's dispensary, but it had already gone under.

Al turned to Tiffany and gave her an exuberant double thumbs-up and a toothy smile where it was obvious that he had been overdoing it on the whitening strips. Tiffany turned in the opposite direction, pretending she didn't see that terrible flash of teeth. Wearing black yoga pants and a pink yoga top, she also pretended not to notice the young guy on the treadmill next to her— with the strong jaw and his hat turned backwards—checking her out.

Meanwhile, by the free weights in the far corner of the gym, a crowd had gathered around one of the flat benches where iron clanked against iron.

Tiffany turned back to Al, sweat drenching the front of his white t-shirt and his chest hair sprouting like gray weeds from the neckline. For a forty-six-year-old guy, he was still in good shape. He drank protein shakes and snacked on raw vegetables. His arms were toned and muscular; if not for the archaic barbed wire armband tattoo that was cool twenty years ago, he could pass for thirty-eight. And the fact that he had a nice pension from the fire department—Tiffany never paid any time they went out—was another bonus of dating a forty-six year old man.

But Al's daughter, who was eighteen and about to graduate high school, was closer to Tiffany's age than Al. Was she going to be Alyssa's stepmother? What about Eloise, Al's ex-wife and her former English teacher? Was Tiffany only a pretty jigsaw piece in Al's aforementioned midlife crisis?

Or is Nate having issues with his own middle-age and projecting through his characters?

Sometimes, especially when they were having sex, Tiffany would look at Al and see the young man buried beneath the layer of worn skin, and it made her want to cry.

The young guy on the treadmill, who barely sweated, winked at Tiffany. She smiled back and imagined it would be nice to be with a man who didn't have to talk to his dick, who wasn't close to scheduling a colonoscopy.

The crowd around the weight bench grew.

With ten minutes left in their forty-minutes of cardio, Tiffany signaled for Al to take out his ear buds. Al complied. "What's up, babe?"

"I think we need to talk."

"Right now?"

"Right now."

The crowd in the free weight section started grew as more forty-five-pound plates clanked against each other, mass on mass, steel on steel.

Confused, Al looked at Tiffany then his eyes rolled back and he fell off the elliptical machine, his body hitting to the floor. Tiffany screamed and jumped off the machine, kneeling beside Al and holding his head in her lap. "Somebody help!"

The gym employees rushed to Al as the crowd by the free weight section parted and a man with a bald dome and inky black hair pulled into a tight ponytail hopped off the weight bench and beat the employees to the scene. The Seagull lifted Al into his arms and carried him to the front lobby. Tiffany followed them.

"What are you doing?" she asked The Seagull.

"'An aged man is but a paltry thing, a tattered coat upon a stick,'" said The Seagull. "And sometimes they talk to their dick."

"Where are you taking him?" Tiffany asked.

"I'm taking him home," The Seagull said.

And everyone watched as The Seagull, carrying an unconscious Al, sprouted billowy white wings from his shoulders blades and flew into a cloudless sky on an otherwise mundane Monday morning. And Al would be okay, and Tiffany and Eloise, too.

But the young guy with his hat on backwards, he was a premature ejaculator.

A Streetcar Named The Seagull

Aleister Bowman was buzzed—not bombed, but buzzed—by the time they reached the climatic Scene 10 of *A Streetcar Named Desire*, which he was directing for The Northboro Community Players. Once a prominent English professor at Northboro College, Aleister slipped away one semester with his office things packed in a cardboard box, head over heels in love with his former student, Miguel. Miguel was neither Hispanic nor Latino. Miguel was actually a Protestant, and his given name was Michael. But he assumed—perhaps correctly—that with his dark complexion, high cheekbones and strong chin, "Miguel" sounded more exotic for the stage and his budding acting career. Now Aleister, adding his own twist to the Tennessee Williams' classic, cast Miguel in his first lead role as Blanche, a decision that prompted all the actresses in The Northboro Community Players to storm off the set, citing favoritism.

The lights were off, and the actors took their places on stage. The crowd, which consisted of a dozen drag queens and half a dozen theater students, murmured to one another, curious to see how Aleister and his all-male cast would execute the rape scene.

Miguel stood center-stage in a red seersucker suit and a rhinestone tiara, sifting through a trunk of clothes, as the spotlight snapped on.

"Are you nervous, Aleister?" asked a stagehand, an unctuous queer with an enlarged forehead named Lorne.

"Get me a martini," Aleister said. "I need a drink." Lately, things with Miguel had been tumultuous, Miguel accusing Aleister of being an insensitive, controlling alcoholic. Earlier in the day, Miguel threatened to not show up for Opening Night, but the threat proved hollow.

Stanley's shadow appeared on a screen in the background—not large and imposing, or sweaty and bestial—rather a different kind of "desire." Aleister's Stanley Kowalski had a bald dome and inky black hair pulled into a tight ponytail. He appeared on stage wearing a turquoise tracksuit.

The Seagull offered a different angle to the character. While he had a background as performance poet, The Seagull's only theater experience was a bit role as the bird in Susan Glaspell's "Trifles." But on Opening Night, The Seagull had captivated the audience, nailing his lines, transforming into an ambiguously gay polymorph named Stanley Kowalski.

In the spotlight, Miguel as Blanche tied a large feathered boa around his neck as Stanley the Seagull approached.

"Just you and me, Blanche," Stanley the Seagull said, hovering over Miguel as Blanche. "Unless you got somebody hid under the bed. What've you got on those fine feathers for?"

"Oh, that's right. You left before the wire," Miguel as Blanche said.

As the two actors worked through the scene, Aleister slammed his vodka martini and began to weep, feeling the full extent of Blanche's helplessness, her dissociation with the primitive modern world. One of the drag queens in the audience stood up and screamed, "Somebody stop that beast."

Stanley the Seagull unzipped the top of the tracksuit, dropped it on the stage and exited left. By the time he returned, he'd opened a beer and changed into bright red velvet pajamas. The characters moved into the bedroom, and Miguel as Blanche smashed a bottle on the table and held it to Stanley the Seagull's face. Miguel as Blanche swung the bottle but Stanley the Seagull caught his arm. "Tiger—tiger! Drop the bottle top. Drop it! We've had this date with each other from the beginning," Stanley the Seagull said, snarling.

Then Stanley the Seagull lifted Miguel as Blanche into his arms, and to Aleister's amazement, he broke script. The top to the bright red velvet pajamas split open and billowy white wings sprouted from The Seagull's shoulder blades. "You will be controlled no more," The Seagull said and ran down the center aisle with Miguel in his arms. The Seagull kicked open the theater's double-doors and flew into the low hazy clouds, swooning in front of the moon on a mild summer night.

Aleister dropped his new drink, the glass smashing on the ground.

"What just happened?" asked Lorne, the sycophantic stagehand.

"Art," said Aleister, wiping a tear from the corner of his eye. "That was art."

Cribbage on Good Friday

You're in your grandfather's kitchen, and it's exactly as you remember it—the table with the glass ring stains on the varnish, the black plastic ashtrays, the walls stained yellow by the nicotine. There's a cuckoo clock next to a small wooden sign that reads: *I've been on a Beer Diet. I've lost three days already.* The cribbage board lies between you and your grandfather on the table.

"It's your crib, Papa," you say.

He raises a Rolling Rock can to his lips. "Do you know how many beaches I stormed in the South Pacific?" he asks, although he's never spoken about the war to you or anyone else for that matter. "Do you know how many goddamn Japs tried to gut me?"

You want to reprimand him for the slur but he's ninety-two years old and he has seen what he's seen. "I can't imagine," you say. "It's your crib, Papa."

"Today's Good Friday," your grandfather says and lights an unfiltered Lucky Strike. Your grandfather, who has already been to the morning and afternoon masses at St. Anthony's, reminds you that Jesus died on the cross at three o'clock today as those Roman thugs watched The Lord suffer. He reminds you of the earthquakes that followed.

"Papa, it's your crib."

Your grandfather's liver-spotted hands, his long fingers crooked and stiff, reach for the cards. He draws on his cigarette while examining this hand. Meanwhile, in the living room, his girlfriends—who wear dark dresses past their knees and stoles made from rabbit fur—are in black and white, sipping gin and tonics. They're holding stalks of yellowish-green palms in their hands. Your grandfather chuckles. "Fifteen four and a double run of three for twelve. Put that in your pipe," he says and laughs and coughs.

"What are your girlfriends doing in the living room, Papa?"

"Waiting," he says.

"For what?" you ask.

"For me."

At three o'clock, the cuckoo bird comes bolting out of the hatch. Only it's not a cuckoo bird, rather a miniature man with a bald dome and inky black hair pulled into a tight ponytail and tiny billowy white wings sprouting from his shoulder blades.

"Namaste," The Seagull says, his hands folded in front of his chest.

Your grandfather rolls his eyes. "Is that some Jap term?"

You start to deal the next hand, the cards facedown, as his girlfriends, in black and white, laugh. Then the scratching of a record needle over vinyl steadies into a song, a big band behind Frank Sinatra singing The Cult's "She Sells Sanctuary." Your grandfather pushes two cards into your crib without looking at them.

The Seagull jumps from his wooden plank on the clock and glides through the kitchen and into the living room where he lands, life-size, beside your grandfather's girlfriends. Your grandmother then appears in the doorway, in color, wearing the leopard skin coat your grandfather bought her when he came back from the war and they were first married, long before his girlfriends.

With his head hanging like it is on hinges, your grandfather cuts the deck, and you flip the five of hearts. Meanwhile, your grandmother, in her coat, hops into The Seagull's arms. The Seagull turns toward the door, kicks open the screen and flies away as the earth shakes from the cataclysm outside.

When you turn back to the table, your grandfather is dead, bullet holes in his chest. His cards are laid out in front of him: three fives and the Jack of Hearts—the perfect hand. The girlfriends make for the door. You try to cry but blood drips from your eyes.

"He's dead," you whisper. "He's finally dead."

Taco Tuesday at the Clear Waters Center

Adam is back at the Clear Waters Center, a mental health facility in downtown Northboro. He was sent there for the first time six months ago after a nervous breakdown following the demise of his marriage and an incident where he took his teenage daughter Kayla to the St. Patrick's Day parade and swore he watched a man dressed as a leprechaun sprout billowy white wings from his shoulder blades and fly into some storm clouds. No person at the parade could corroborate Adam's account, except for a senile old couple drinking milk from mugs and flatulating. After his first visit, the doctors at The Clear Waters Center diagnosed Adam with Bipolar II and prescribed him Seroquel to stabilize his moods, Celexa for his depression, and Ativan for his pesky panic attacks—a drug cocktail that left him moving through his days zombie-like, emotionless.

Now he's back.

His second breakdown occurred on Saturday night, after his ex-wife Sarah announced her engagement to the Northboro mayor's son Todd LaFleur on Facebook, changing her profile picture to an opulent four-carat rock on her ring finger. Adam snapped. He washed down seven Ativan and seven Seroquel with seven beers in the backseat of Sarah's unlocked Elantra in her driveway, listening to The Cult's "Sweet Soul Sister"—Adam and Sarah's wedding song, if you recall—on repeat.

Adam woke up in the emergency room, unsure how he got there, and watched the leprechaun whisper into a priest's ear. He then fell back asleep and was soon transferred, via ambulance, to the Clear Waters Center.

Now on Tuesday night, during the arts and crafts hour, Adam is making a popsicle-stick Christmas tree using watercolors, Elmer's glue and tiny red and green pom-poms. Halfway through the hour, Joseph, a burly man in his early-sixties with a bulbous nose and a paunch hard enough to dive off, jumps up from his chair and points at Adam.

"Motherfucker," Joseph screams, pointing a stiff index finger in Adam's face. "This motherfucker stole a popsicle-stick from me and now my fucking Christmas tree is fucked!"

Two of the counselors—Mpenda, a tall Kenyan man, and Phil, an aging hippy with a gray beard and round-rimmed glasses—grab Joseph by the arms and hold him back.

"No one stole your popsicle stick, Joseph," Mpenda says in a soothing voice, his accent a massage.

"That motherfucker did," Joseph says, squirming to get at Adam.

Adam shrugs and stares out a picture window at the streetlights and two shabby duplexes. He remembers the duplex he and Sarah rented when they were first married. One Christmas Eve, while living there, Adam brought home a kitten for Kayla, who was six years old. Sarah was working as a waitress at a sports' bar, and when she came home from her shift and saw the kitten with Kayla, she screamed—a good scream, a lungful of mirth—then wept with joy.

Adam turns back and faces Joseph, who is still trying to wrestle his way out the counselors' grips. "Merry Christmas," Adam says and hands him the popsicle-stick that he had shoved up his sleeve.

Joseph throws back his head and roars.

Adam watches as the cook at The Clear Waters Center brings out the whiteboard with the dinner menu. As Joseph reads it, the fury in his face dissolves, and he stops squirming and points at the whiteboard. Adam and the other patients, peeling the glue from their fingertips, watch as Joseph cheers while jumping up and down. "It's Taco Tuesday! It's Taco fucking Tuesday!"

Adam smiles and feels like the main character in a Christmas special that ends with the father and daughter embracing and forgiving all wrongdoings.

Mpenda and Phil release Joseph and he sprints to the dinner line. But someone beats him there. The man in front of Joseph has a bald dome and inky black hair pulled into a tight ponytail.

Joseph balls his fists and stomps his feet, his face again flushed. "The fucking Seagull is always the first on Taco fucking Tuesday!"

Adam steps in the back of the line, awaiting his after-dinner meds, in no hurry to be anywhere. The Seagull looks familiar, of course.

On Taco Tuesday, the choice of tacos is between chicken or beef or beans. The Seagull secures the only piece of haddock and shares his second fish taco with Adam.

Everything Blows Up for The
Andre Whittaker Trio

If Darren were being honest, he would tell you that he never liked Andre Whittaker, the founder and frontman for the Andre Whittaker Jazz Trio, who plays Dave Brubreck covers on Thursday nights in the cocktail lounge at La Carreta's in downtown Northboro. Andre wears a sports coat and a thin tie and these goofy horn-rimmed glasses and...go ahead, Darren. Say it. We know what you're thinking.

"I hate that motherfucker," Darren muttered under his breath as they finished "Take Five" and Darren spun his stand-up bass indifferently on its endpin.

Tall and lanky in his late-forties, Andre Whittaker spoke to the crowd like he'd just finished smoking a joint with Jack Kerouac. "All right, cats. Dig," he said.

An old couple drinking mugs of milk in the back of lounge applauded. Everyone else continued their conversations, the music relegated to ambient noise. The Thursday night crowd in the cocktail lounge consisted largely of middle-aged professionals, doctors and lawyers and engineers—only the engineers drove trains and didn't design buildings or bridges. The engineers wore their blue and white striped train caps, and had pocket watches hanging from their belts.

On that Thursday night, Andre's girlfriend Lydia— who was going through a divorce with husband coming unhinged—sat alone at a two-top, less than ten feet from the piano, sipping a Mimosa and snapping her fingers.

Andre Whittaker tapped on the microphone in 5/4 time. "Dig, daddy-o," Andre said to the crowd as the engineers blew into wooden train whistles.

"Cool, man," said Andre Whittaker as Darren seethed behind him. "Try this on."

Darren and the drummer, a French-Canadian named Guy, worked into the backbeat as Andre soloed on the piano. While he is being honest, Darren wanted to chew off Andre Whittaker's fingers, shave his stupid soul-patch then take a steaming dump inside his piano.

As Darren plucked the bass, there was a commotion in the back of the lounge, and a man was screaming something inaudible. Darren and Guy stopped playing then Andre Whittaker screeched to a halt. A thin man in a red sweater, visibly drunk, was standing on his barstool, his hands cupped over his mouth. "There's a bomb in the piano," he screamed.

"Who is this cat?" Andre Whittaker asked into the microphone.

"There's a bomb in the piano," the man screamed again.

"Not groovy," said Andre Whittaker.

Andre's girlfriend then sprung from her seat, knocking over her Mimosa. "Oh my God, Lewis! What the fuck are you doing here?"

It didn't take Darren long to figure out that the man shouting the bomb threat was Lydia's estranged husband. From the corner of his eye, he watched Andre Whittaker open the lid to the piano and peek inside then jump back as if a snake lashed at him. "There *is* a bomb in there!"

Now here was Darren's dilemma: In his late-twenties, Darren had worked briefly with a bomb squad and could certainly detonate the bomb with the sure-handed swiftness of a surgeon. Yet, if he kept quiet, they would evacuate the room, no one would get hurt and Andre Whittaker's dumb fucking piano would blow up. As Darren contemplated his options, one of engineers came jogging toward the stage area. He tossed off his cap, revealing a bald dome and inky black hair pulled into a tight ponytail.

"Move aside," The Seagull said and looked at Darren. "You should remember me."

"Seagull," Darren said. "I always knew it was you. How have you been?"

"Get your ass over here and help me," The Seagull said.

Meanwhile, the other engineers in the lounge placed Lewis under a citizen's arrest, his hands bound with a bar rag. Darren and The Seagull worked together and had the bomb detonated before the police and the bomb squad arrived.

The Seagull shook Darren's hand while Andre Whittaker got on one knee and proposed to Lydia, indifferent to the fact that she was still legally married to the man who tried to blow him up.

"It was great seeing you again," Darren said to The Seagull.

"Namaste, Darren," The Seagull said and folded his hands in front of his heart. "Go easy on that cat." The Seagull tilted his head toward Andre Whittaker, who was still on his knee with a look like he'd been stumped in trivia. Then The Seagull went back to the table with the other engineers and ordered the fish tacos.

Eventually, the show went on. The show always goes on.

The Toast

Matt Rogers was shit-faced at Tony and Allison's wedding reception at The Northboro Country Club. In the years since high school, Matt and Tony became friends, an unlikely alliance, and now Matt Rogers—the bully from the former stories—was Tony's best man and about to give a speech.

Allison's sister Isabella had just finished a perfectly innocuous and saccharine Maid of Honor Address, replete with soft laughs and platitudes. Fighting back tears, Isabella explained how Allison wasn't only her big sister but her best friend, too.

Some women in the crowd wiped the corners of their eyes with the linen napkins.

Matt Rogers then snatched the microphone from Isabella and whacked it against his open palm, blowing into it and screaming, "Is this thing on?"

Allison turned to Tony at the wedding party's table in the front of the banquet hall, her eyes blowtorches. "Maybe we should stop him," she said.

"He's fine," Tony said. "Maybe he'll say something interesting and spice up this story."

"Maybe we should stop him." Allison picked up a pineapple from the fruit tray in front of them and held it with her arm cocked, her crosshairs aimed at Matt Rogers.

Tony grabbed her arm. "For god's sake, Allison, not the pineapple," he said. "Matt might say something interesting, albeit stupid. It's really up to Nate."

Allison eased down the pineapple. "I hope Nate doesn't allow Matt Rogers to ruin our reception."

"Nate calls the shots. These are his stories."

"What if I buy him a drink?" Allison asked, desperate.

Tony sighed. "Nate does like to drink, but you never can tell."

Meanwhile, Matt Rogers karate-kicked the air in front of him and folded his hands together in front of his heart and bowed. "Namaste, motherfuckers," he said. "I want to start by saying it's great to see The Pelican getting married, guaranteed poon-tang for the rest of his life."

The room fell silent, save a few gasps and the clatter of silverware in the back of the banquet hall. "Seriously, folks," Matt said then belched into the microphone, "I've known Tony since elementary school, and for the longest time I shit on him because of his huge honker. But then, after some dickhead janitor smashed my nose, I started to empathize with The Pelican and came to see him as a real person. Soon he became my friend, and now I'm his best man. Fucked up, right? But I remember this one time, Tony and me went out with a couple of slam pigs. I mean, half the dudes in this room have run train on these chicks. But I let Tony choose which one he wanted to nail first. If that's not friendship, what is?"

"Make him stop," Allison said to her new husband. "Matt is about to tell another lie."

"I can't," Tony said, grabbing her hand. "Only Nate can stop him."

"I hate it when Nate does this. Nate, stop Matt Rogers before he tells another stupid lie," she begged of me.

But, Allison, I can't. My job is to make this story more interesting.

"But Tony is much more than a man with a huge beak," Matt Rogers continued. "He is also a guy who forgives an ass-ton when it comes to his friends. I mean, who out of the groomsmen hasn't laid some pipe with the bride? Allison even gave me a tuggy after the rehearsal dinner last night. No biggie. The Pelican forgives."

Then a waiter with a bald dome and inky black pulled into a tight ponytail walked up behind Matt Rogers and delivered a swift roundhouse kick to the back of his head.

Matt Rogers dropped like a sack of birdfeed, knocked out cold. The Seagull then pointed out the picture window of the banquet hall. Outside, beyond the rolling green and the soft sloping hills on the golf course, simmering above a line of pine trees on the horizon, pelicans and seagulls swooned in and out of the clouds in the orange dusk.

I'd like to make The Pelican sprout billowy wings from his shoulder blades and make The Seagull and The Pelican smash through the windows and join their fellow birds in flight.

But I can't.

Who would believe it?

But I will tell you that Tony and Allison are still married, raising kids who are functional—which is the best any of us can do with kids—and they never again talked to Matt Rogers, who died of dick cancer.

A Day at Dr. Dick Doyle's
Male Enhancement Clinic

Recently divorced, Seth surveyed the waiting room at Dr. Dick Doyle's Male Enhancement Clinic, a small office space burrowed in a strip mall, wedged between a questionable massage parlor and a law firm specializing in personal injury. The bald and balding men in the waiting room kept their gazes down, flipping through old copies of *Maxim*. Seth was sitting next to man who simply stared at his hands.

Seth realized everyone in the waiting room must've watched Dr. Dick Doyle's late-night commercials during syndicated episodes of *Seinfeld*, where Dr. Doyle promised "to re-grow hair" while "adding genital enhancement for [their] lady friends." In the commercial, Dr. Doyle—a plump and red-faced man in his sixties with a head full of jet-black hair and an obvious kielbasa shoved into his pair of ill-fitting pleated Dockers—stood next to buxom blonde nurse as he stared into the camera and deadpanned: "Do you feel ill-equipped to satisfy your woman? Is your male-pattern baldness making you self-conscious? Come in to Dr. Dick Doyle's Male Enhancement Clinic for a free consultation. We'll grow your hair and help you down there."

The nurse from the commercial with bleached hair and cantaloupe-sized breast augmentations opened the door to the waiting room. She wore a skimpy uniform that could've passed as a Halloween costume with a white, low-cut blouse and a thigh-high skirt and black fishnet stockings. A paper visor with a red cross on the front completed the ensemble. "Mr. Cain, we're ready for you," she said in a raspy, sultry voice.

Seth and the other bald men broke into applause, patting Mr. Cain—a pear-shaped guy with coke-bottle glasses—on the back as he jogged to the office door. "Remember me," Mr. Cain shouted to the other men as the nurse rubbed his bald head like she were petting a small dog, and they disappeared, the door closing behind them.

A man across from Seth, who was reading an issue of *Maxim* with Scarlett Johannson on the cover in a slinky silver dress, whistled one long low-note. "I don't know about you, but I'm sick of this Jason Alexander-shit," the man said to Seth. "I'm ready to rock and roll again."

"I don't understand," Seth said, although he did. They had both watched the same commercial during the same television program.

"He's the actor who plays George Costanza on *Seinfeld*, the bald guy."

"Who is that?" Seth asked.

The man snorted and lowered his head, aggressively flipping the pages of the magazine. But Seth was in no mood for small talk. Since his divorce with Melanie, who took full-custody of their kids, his younger girlfriend left him for the lead singer of The Cult cover band called The American Horse—damn, her new boyfriend had a rocking head of hair. Meanwhile, Melanie had moved in with a high school science teacher at Northboro High School who treated her and his kids with the kindness and patience and concern she deserved. So Seth didn't need this bald man's dull banter. Seth needed to grow his hair and elongate his cock. Then the women would flock to him like groupies…no, that's a bad analogy for Seth. The women would flock to him like…birds?

The nurse reappeared, her lipstick smeared. "Seagull, we're ready for you," she said in her huskiest husky voice.

A guy with a bald dome and inky black pulled into a tight ponytail stood up from the back of the waiting room. "Are you *really* ready?" The Seagull asked the nurse.

"I always knew it was you," the nurse said and took his hand, and the two tangoed toward the office exit, and The Seagull sprouted billowy white wings from his shoulder blades, and the nurse jumped into his arms and they flew off. Everyone in the waiting room, with the exception of Seth, stood and applauded then formed a Conga line out the door.

So Seth sat alone in the waiting room and picked up the copy of *Maxim* the man across from him was reading. The cover was white, image-less. Scarlett Johannson left, too.

Jed's Big Birthday Bash

For Jed's twenty-first birthday, his best friend Willy and his cousin Larry took him to The Pits, a biker bar on the outskirts of Northboro. The Pits had horseshoe sandpits and recently installed a couple of cornhole boards where the patrons drank and played outside until dark.

The three men drove in Larry's truck. Larry and Willy were both twenty-two and had a little more experience at bars than Jed, who had none. In fact, Jed had never touched a drop of alcohol. As the vice president of the 4-H Club, he felt the need to lead by example. Jed had also never had sex. He once felt up Gail, the 4-H Club vice-president, when she was going through a divorce, but it never went past a squeeze of her breasts over the bra. And Jed sure as hell never smoked weed, although he once got a contact high hanging out with a couple of carnies at The Northboro County Fair.

It was a Thursday night, and some gruff looking bikers were sitting at the bar, leather-vested and bearded and beer-bellied. The three young men sat in the stools beside them. Willy eavesdropped on their conversation.

"Fuck you, Brian. *Lear* is by far the saddest of Shakespeare's tragedies," a biker with a thick red beard said. "You have a broken senile old man whose daughters betray him. *Hamlet,* my hairy red ass."

"So you're just going to dismiss poor Ophelia, you fishmonger," said the other biker who had a handlebar mustache and rust-colored eyes.

"Call me a fishmonger again, and I'll punch you in the fucking throat."

"You have no soul, Allen."

The three young men ordered a pitcher of Bud Light then moved to a booth with a boar's head mounted above them. Willy's goal was to get so drunk that the boar's head spoke to him. You see, Willy had a bad week, a week stolen from a country music song: The transmission in his Chevy dropped like a bucket of pig guts; the girl he was dating broke it off with him to be with the front man of a Johnny Cash cover band called A Boy Named Sue; and his dog, Cracker—while he didn't go missing—had a mighty case of the runs that had Willy in and out of the laundry mat.

Yes, Willy needed to get drunk.

Once Jed's palate adapted to the taste of beer, he started seriously pounding. He had three glasses to Willy's two. Poor Larry, who was driving, only had half a mug of Bud Light when they ordered a second pitcher. Willy then bought a round of Kamikaze shots, and the next thing they knew, Jed was drunk—shit-faced, hammered, shammered, blitzed, obliterated, ossified, annihilated, toasted, wrecked.

At a table across from their booth, two girls were staring at the boar's head. Jed catcalled at them, and a blonde with a white bow in her hair looked at him, steely-eyed, and said, "Is there something you'd like to say?"

"You look like healthy women," Jed slurred. "I bet you could saddle a bull."

The bikers stepped in front of the girls. "Knave," said the biker with the handlebar mustache, pointing at Jed. "How dare you dishonor these maidens. I'm about to jam my steel-toed boot up your ass, junior."

Willy looked a Larry, who was laughing at the boar's head telling a knock-knock joke, prompting Willy to look up at the boar's head, too.

"Impatient cow," cried the boar's head. "Moo!"

The red-bearded biker slipped on a set of brass knuckles and started toward Jed when he was kicked in the back of the head and dropped like a bucket of squirrel guts. In front of the booth, between the young men and the girls, stood a guy with a bald dome and inky black hair pulled into a tight ponytail.

"Seagull!" Willy said. "Where did you come from?"

"Nate wrote me into the story to save your asses," The Seagull said as the other biker charged him from behind, and The Seagull dropped him like a bucket of oxen entrails with an elbow to the chin.

Jed smiled the gassy smile of the newly inebriated. "That was damn nice of Nate," Jed said. "Can I buy him a beer?"

"Of course you can," said The Seagull.

"Namaste," said Jed to The Seagull.

"Namaste, Jed," The Seagull said then turned to Willy and bowed, his hand pressed in front of his heart. "Namaste, Larry. Namaste, Willy."

With tears streaming down his cheeks, Willy pressed his hands together and bowed. "Namaste, Seagull."

The girls protested at their table. "But Nate can't make us go home with you creeps," said the blonde with the white bow.

"Of course he can," said Larry, speaking for the first time in the story. "He's the writer. He can do anything."

But I did no such thing, and as they were leaving the bar, Jed leaned over and puked on the cornhole board, straight through the chute without splattering any vomit on the wood. And if you don't think that's impressive, try it yourself.

And me? I drank Jed's beer. After all, he was buying.

The Sweethearts of The Class of 1993

When Jason received the invitation for the reunion, he thought they had the wrong address. But, sure enough, it was addressed specifically to him, even using his middle initial, which was R for Regan—his father was an extra in the protest scene of *The Exorcist*. The invitation said that Northboro High School's Class of 1993 would "be honored" if Jason attended, yet Jason still had no recollection of living in Northboro, much less attending the high school. But he enjoyed putting on a suit and dabbing on cologne and applying gel in his hair. And Jason enjoyed reunions—they brought back some of what his amnesia wiped clean—so he sent back the envelope to the reunion committee affirming that he would be attending.

Upon arrival, however, Jason found himself standing at the end of a bar in the banquet hall of The Northboro Country Club, restless and bored. The deejay, with his equipment set up in the back of the room behind a parquet dance floor, wore banana-yellow MC Hammer pants and spun his antique Los Angeles Raider's hat backwards. He was playing "Ice, Ice, Baby" and hopping around in the deejay booth. Jason could not remember ever feeling more alone than he did standing at that bar, in his only suit, smiling at people he didn't recognize in the dimmed lighting.

"I never thought I'd see you here," said a stranger with broad shoulders and a helmet of gray hair as he clapped Jason on the shoulder. "Amanda said you wouldn't show. But look at this, the class sweethearts have arrived."

"In the flesh," Jason said and smiled at the stranger. "Can I buy you something to drink?"

"Just a Diet Coke," the stranger said. "You remember what I was like. If there was a superlative for 'Most Likely to End Up in AA' I would've had that locked."

"Good for you for getting sober," Jason said.

"It was that or go to jail," the man shrugged.

A group of men dressed in Northboro High School Seahawks jerseys were standing around the dance floor, drinking beer in bottles and staring at Jason.

A woman wearing a strapless blue prom dress approached Jason. Her teeth were gritted, her nostrils flaring. She punched him in the chest. "You chickenshit, asshole, son of a bitch, dick-hole! How dare you!" She punched him again.

"Please stop."

The woman punched him a third time then kneed him in the groin. "What about your daughter!"

"What daughter?" Jason asked, hunched over and gasping for breath.

"Her name is Hannah, you asshole. We had her our senior year!"

"I don't remember."

By now, The Class of 1993 had formed a semicircle around them, everyone hissing at Jason. Amanda, in a histrionic fit, flung her arm over her eyes and feigned fainting, collapsing to her knees then falling to floor. "And to think," she said, lifting her head, "we were the Class Sweethearts in 1993."

The Class of 1993 then lined up, single-file, a line that stretched the perimeters of the banquet hall, and they each took a turn hissing in Jason's face, one at a time. The men dressed in the Seahawk jerseys were the last in line, and the final guy had a bald dome and inky black hair pulled into a tight ponytail. Jason recognized him from a homecoming football game that fall.

"You have to try these bacon-wrapped scallops," The Seagull said and held out a plate.

"I remember you," Jason said and took one of the bacon-wrapped scallops. "I always knew it was you."

"I was voted Most Likely to Fly," The Seagull said and popped the last bacon-wrapped scallop into his mouth. "What do you think of the scallops?"

"They're delicious," Jason said and somehow he knew he'd remember the taste of that scallop and The Seagull's small act of kindness when everyone else hissed at him. You remember those kinds of things— even with amnesia.

Fire Woman

Thomas—the pretentious little prick who endured The Northboro Atomic Wedgy in the lunch line in the previous section—legally changed his name to Tomas after college while trying to reinvent himself as a literary scholar. Now he sat on a red velour couch in the VIP room of The Dirty Bird beside his future brother-in-law Bobby, whose smile stretched from one clubbed ear to the other as a buxom brunette rubbed her breasts against Bobby's face. Meanwhile, a blonde stripper with smoky eyes ground her ass against Tomas's crotch as he shifted in his seat, attempting to readjust his tiny erection so it wasn't blatantly protruding in his beige pleated Dockers.

Truth be told, Tomas found the black lights and the scent of cheap lavender perfume, mixed with sweaty desperation, lurid and obscene. If Bobby, who was pickled on draft beer and Southern Comfort, hadn't dragged Tomas into this room, there would be no way he would have subjected himself to such unfettered filth and an embarrassing arousal.

The first song—The Cult's "Wake Up Time for Freedom"—ended, signifying the completion of the first half of the two-song contract Bobby had brokered with the strippers. Tomas cleared his throat as the stripper, who performed under the stage name of Lexus, stepped back and unfastened her bra, allowing it to fall to the ground between her red stiletto heels. Always an aficionado of proportions, Tomas had to admit her breasts were exceptional. Meanwhile, his microphallus swelled, reducing him to a mouth-breathing, ear-scratching, finger-sniffing brute like his future brother-in-law.

The erection disconcerted Tomas to the point where he decided to shift gears with the vixen.

"I don't suppose you're familiar with Yeats," Tomas said. He had recently graduated with a bachelor's degree in Literature—with a capital L—from Northboro College and was tearing his way through the Modernists, rereading Yeats' *The Tower*. Yet Tomas had a soul like a block of tofu and seldom felt any of what he read; instead, the douche bag processed the words, analyzed the language and metaphor, and commented copiously on diction and syntax, priding himself as a New Critic. But as far as feeling the magic on the page, the ineffable vibration poetry produced in the deepest and darkest untouched crevasses of the self, Tomas was oblivious. In short, he was the kind of guy you'd like to punch in the mouth for the simple reason that his face—clean-shaven to the point where you questioned if he grew facial hair, with his thick, puckered red lips—was supremely punchable, and his haughtiness only added to the effect.

As Tomas was thinking douchey things about the feminine mystique, the song "Fire Woman" blasted through the speakers mounted in the four corners of the room. Lexus swayed her hips. "I'm a doctoral student in comparative studies," she said to Tomas without meeting his beady little eyes. "I'm writing my dissertation on Modernist poetry. '"Things fall apart,"' she added, glancing at his pathetic erection, "'the centre cannot hold; mere anarchy is loosed upon the world.'"

Tomas—to use a vulgar idiom he'd despise—nearly soiled his shorts as Lexus' hips moved to the driving beat of rock n' roll. Never had Tomas experienced such a paroxysm of pure lust, such a Wordsworthian spontaneous overflow of blood and desire filling his groin. Lexus tugged at the sides of her red g-string and straddled Tomas's lap. If she felt his diminutive boner—which was highly unlikely—she didn't acknowledge it. Tomas's vision blurred and his breathing quickened. Before he knew what he was doing, his hands reached for Lexus's breasts.

As soon as his fingertips grazed her nipple, a man with a bald dome and inky black hair pulled into a tight ponytail burst into the room. He jumped into the air and landed a solid spin-kick to Tomas' jaw, knocking Tomas onto the floor. As Tomas lay dazed, rubbing his chin, his bowels released a long zipper-like rip of gas. "The worst are full of passionate intensity," Tomas said.

His future brother-in-law laughed. Truth be told, Bobby couldn't stand Tomas, the smug little fuck. "That was bitchin'," Bobby said to The Seagull. "You were like Steven Seagal."

"Close," The Seagull said. "There's no touching the dancers. Now, Bobby, take him home."

"You got it, Seagull," Bobby said, nudging Tomas with his foot. "Get up, Fart-boy. We're leaving."

The Seagull smiled at Bobby and pointed to Tomas. "He's lucky Nate didn't have him killed. Nate can't stand him," said The Seagull.

And it's true: I can't stand Tomas, and while I don't typically kill characters—except for Matt Rogers—I did give Tomas a microphallus and indefatigable flatulence.

Intermission

This is the part of the book where I began to lose my faith in this creation. I've come this far but the initial faith felt when I first saw The Seagull at the bar and he told me that this book "was meant to happen," that faith has waned. Make no bones about it, folks: writing a book is an article of faith that is tested, time and time again, throughout its creation.

At some point in the process, however, the reasonable mind begins to undermine your faith in the book. For example, what happens if no one wants to publish this? Would I still believe that anyone needs to read the story of a modern angel sent to save the lonely denizens of Northboro, my fictional town?

And what if someone agrees to publish the book but no one buys it? Although I suppose it's an auspicious sign that you're reading this now: It means you've made to the end, and we're about to wrap things up with The Seagull.

But how do I end it? I suppose I must have faith that I'll figure it out.

Before I finish this book, I've decided that The Seagull needs to save *me*. I need him to scoop me in his arms as he sprouts billowy white wings from his shoulder blades and fly me away from this solitary place where I write, summoning the faith to finish.

In Love with Harmony

Sean—you remember Sean, that block-headed brick of muscle who kept sending dick-pics to his now ex-wife Rochelle in the vain hope of winning her back—he judiciously gave up on human females after the divorce.

But he had a back-up plan.

With his life's savings, in addition to some prize money he won in a body-building competition in Providence, Sean invested in Harmony, a human-sized sex-bot capable of carrying on conversations through an application on his phone. For nearly twenty-grand, Harmony was built to Sean's specifications—DD breasts, twenty-six-inch waist, curvy hips and a firm ass. Harmony's silicone skin was pale with a subtle blush in her high cheekbones, and she had full glossy lips, an unassuming nose and hypnotic ocean-blue eyes that scanned Sean when she spoke in her Scottish accent. Sean was also able to program her personality to his own emotional predilections—obsequious, not to speak unless spoken to, and perpetually horny. Harmony was the intellectual and emotional antithesis of his ex-wife—if emotions are, indeed, the right terminology to use when dealing with artificial intelligence.

But Sean loved Harmony, and Harmony was programmed to love him.

The last you remember of Sean, he got knocked the out by The Seagull, who was dating Rochelle. But that was long before Harmony arrived via Fed Ex in a large wooden crate with Styrofoam and newspaper chippings and loads and loads of bubble wrap. And since Harmony entered Sean's life, he even made amends with Rochelle, and Rochelle allowed Sean to keep Albert, their Great Dane. In fact, Rochelle was coming for dinner at Sean's apartment to meet Harmony for the first time and enjoy some grilled Sirloin steaks and baked haddock, and drink some wine and protein shakes. Except for Harmony. She doesn't eat or drink because she is a robot.

Sean went to the gym earlier in the day and did chest and triceps, some light cardio on the elliptical machine, and while waiting for Rochelle to arrive, he cranked out a few sets of push-ups in front of the television with Harmony propped up on the couch, her mechanical eyes following him.

"Watch me work up a pump, darling," Sean said.

"What's your favorite muscle group to exercise?" Harmony asked.

"Glad you asked, babe," Sean said, falling on his side and leaning on his elbow, facing Harmony. "I like to pump up my pecks for you."

"Did you know that a gallon of gas cost twenty-six cents in 1972," said Harmony.

"I love it when you talk dirty."

"Want to hear a dirty joke?" Harmony asked. "A white horse fell in a mud puddle."

"That's great, baby," Sean said and flexed a bicep for his sex-bot. "Look at these pipes."

"Glass pipes are a preferred method for smoking marijuana among many users, although vaporizing and marijuana edibles are gaining popularity," said Harmony.

The doorbell rang, and Sean adjusted Harmony on the couch, a silicone leg propped up on a cushion, her straight blonde hair parted at the side and falling on her shoulders. Sean stopped for a moment to admire her beauty, her perfect proportions; to admire the fact that unlike his ex-wife, Harmony was never contentious, never disagreed and completely supported Sean's bodybuilding and the time and resources it required. Veins bulging in his biceps, Sean answered the door.

When he opened it, Rochelle was holding a bottle of Amoretto and standing beside the guy with the bald dome and inky black hair pulled into a tight ponytail.

"What's that pussy doing here?" Sean said, pointing at The Seagull.

From the living room, Harmony said, "Pussy Galore was a character from Ian Fleming's 1959 James Bond novel *Goldfinger*. She would later be played in the 1964 film adaptation by the actress Honor Blackman."

Upon hearing the programmed Scottish accent and catching a glimpse of Sean's sex-bot on the couch, Rochelle dropped the bottle of Amoretto, shattering it on the front steps. "What the fuck is that?" Rochelle asked.

"That's my baby girl," Sean said, grinning. "Get a load of this hot piece of ass. Unlike some people I've lived with, Harmony never bitches and is *always* down to fuck."

The Seagull then knocked Sean back with a straight-legged kick to the chest and ran into the living room. He scooped Harmony in his arms as billowy white wings sprouted from his shoulder blades. Sean could only watch as The Seagull grabbed his ex-wife's hand, set her on his back and flew away with Rochelle and Harmony into a dark cloud covering a full moon.

From his living room floor, Sean's muscles shrunk and deflated until he was skin and bones. Then the skin and then the bones disappeared, too. And *poof*. Sean was gone from the book.

The Nightmare in Northboro

Donald took four Xanax from the prescription Dr. Belmont write for his recently deceased mother, Priscilla. After the passing of her parakeet Nugget— and her philandering husband Dick, who was barely in the hole when the bird died—Priscilla succumbed to a depression that her heart couldn't withstand, leaving Donald alone in his deceased parents' home with some life decisions to face.

He decided to start by confronting the agoraphobia that kept him from leaving the house. Urged by members of his Facebook support group and fortified by an ass-ton of benzos, Donald drove his parents' car to *The Nightmare in Northboro*, a haunted house one Yelp reviewer described as "shit your shorts scary."

Another reviewer wrote: *There's nothing as sad as a starving black cat.*

Donald designed the trip as a form of shock therapy, his means of breaking out of his parents' house and making his own way in an already-terrifying world.

After waiting in a forty-five-minute line, he entered the rickety wooden house and squeezed through a narrow hallway, flustered and fanning himself with his hands. Donald then found himself in a room the size of a gas station bathroom with a strobe light flickering in the corner. There was a card-table in the center of the room with a bloody rubber head as its centerpiece, its mouth mid-scream. Donald meant to scream himself but instead he mumbled, "Nugget."

Earlier that day, his online girlfriend Danielle, who was slated to finally meet Donald in person and join him at *The Nightmare in Northboro*, informed him that she could no longer cyber-date a carnivore. Dejected, Donald shook his head while he typed: *smh*. His father Dick was the deli manager for three decades—for three decades Dick handled the meat—and Donald couldn't budge on his position. *I love you*, he wrote, *but the meat is part of me*.

For some reason, Danielle stopped responding.

As Donald was staring at the bloody rubber head and thinking about Danielle and the meat and his mother and Nugget, a man wearing a plastic squirrel mask jumped into the room revving a bladeless chainsaw.

Donald meant to scream but instead he yawned.

The man in the squirrel mask cackled maniacally. "I'll have a pound of bratwurst, half a pound of bologna and two Xanax, Donald," he said in a forced high-pitched voice.

"I know you," Donald said.

"No one knows The Squirrel," he said.

"You're not The Squirrel. You're The Seagull."

"You always knew," said The Seagull and ripped off his squirrel mask revealing a bald dome and inky black hair pulled into a tight ponytail.

The people waiting in line that night swore they saw something fly out of the haunted house. Some said it was a bat, while others argued that it was too big to be a bat. Still, other folks swore that they saw billowy white wings sprout from a human form and feathers fell like raindrops on the line as the form flew away holding someone else in his arms. An old couple drinking mugs of milk claimed someone broke through the exit and scampered up a tree.

As The Seagull flew toward the crescent moon, with Donald in his arms, Donald muttered, "Nugget."

"How do you feel?" The Seagull asked him.

Donald looked down at the earth. "I've never felt better."

The Last Goodbye

Before the divorce paperwork was finalized, Rocco and Lauren decided to spend one last night together. They made a reservation at a four-star restaurant in downtown Northboro, a seafood place called The Lobster's Grille then they hit the bars they once frequented when they were young and falling in love. Rocco and Lauren got drunk together then walked back, hand-in-hand, to the Northboro Inn where they had booked a room.

"Do you think we did the right thing?" Lauren asked Rocco as they stepped beneath a streetlight, their shadows stretching on the sidewalk.

Rocco shrugged and removed his Red Sox hat and placed it on Lauren's head. "I want you to have this," he said.

With pressure built behind Lauren's eyes, she blinked, hard and fast, and fought back tears. "I can't," she said.

"You must," Rocco said.

Outside their room, Rocco fumbled with the keycard, and as soon as they entered, they were on each other, their bodies spilling on the satin sheets. Lauren unbuckled Rocco's belt, and Rocco unhitched her bra. "Tonight feels magical," he whispered into his soon-to-be ex-wife's ear. "It's like we're young again."

"We can still change our minds," Lauren said between heavy breathes.

"If only," Rocco said. He knew, short of a miracle, this was the last time he'd ever touch her body, a body he'd come to know, over twenty years together, as well as his own; this was the last time he'd rub her small shoulders or massage her heavy breasts; the last time he'd feel her quiver, her bones vibrating as she climaxed. And a sadness, a longing and a lament, washed over him as he entered Lauren and she moaned like a door creaking open.

With Rocco inside her, Lauren remembered their honeymoon in Aruba, the tinder box hotel room and the deep scent of tobacco in the lobby. Rocco had told her that she'd be the last woman he'd ever love as they lay sweating beneath the cheap cotton sheets, a ceiling fan whirling, and the sun—an orange orb—setting on the beach outside that room's only window.

Yet tonight, in their inexact ways, and how much they were going to miss one another and their memories together—even the pain and the betrayals—these were living parts of them now. Separately, they thought about their wedding day, a small gathering in their backyard with their drunken friends and humorless families; and they thought about the way they looked at one another that day of their wedding and communicated with simple lifts of their eyebrows.

Then they looked at each other that way again and tried to say their goodbyes.

As they were switching from a missionary position, Lauren started to quiver. "Don't stop," she said.

"Keep your hand right there," Rocco said.

Then they both stopped and stared at each other, their eyebrows asking questions.

"My hand isn't on you," Lauren said.

"I'm not inside you," said Rocco.

As Rocco looked up, and Lauren glanced over her shoulder, they saw billowy white wings sprouting, the width of the king-sized mattress. A man with a bald dome and inky black hair pulled into a tight ponytail stood tall on the foot of the bed.

Rocco sat up, and Lauren placed her arms around her husband. "Seagull," Lauren said. "I always knew it was you."

"What are you doing here?" Rocco asked.

"Saving your marriage," The Seagull said. "Namaste, Rocco."

"Namaste, Seagull," Rocco said and pressed his face into Lauren's bare shoulder, and she lifted his chin and kissed his lips.

The Seagull then flew out the open window and across the Northboro skyline, looking down at the city lights and the people walking the streets, the people lonely and estranged from a faith that could save them. And The Seagull became a silhouette with his billowy white wings sprouting from his shoulder blades in the backdrop of the moon's pale light.

And there you have it: a happy ending.

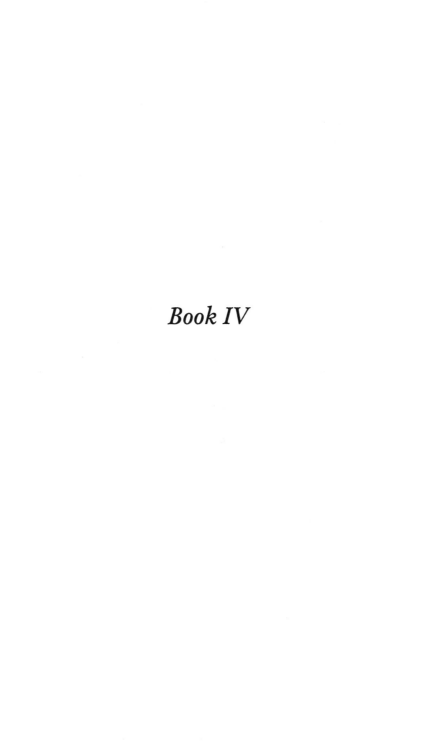

Book IV

The Son of The Seagull

Somewhere on the outskirts of the Northboro, a log cabin stands in the woods. The cabin is far from extravagant, a single unadorned room with bare walls and a wood stove in the corner, a generator that runs on propane, a futon bed and a bookshelf that includes hardcover editions of *Walden* and The Bible. In back of the cabin, there's an outhouse where the eight published books of poetry and prose by Nate Graziano are stacked on a single shelf beside the hole—just in case.

A crib made of maple with a mobile of birds spinning in the musty air was recently erected beside the futon.

Here, as winter approaches, the trees that shade the house from April through October have shed their leaves, and piles of rustic reds and browns, yellows and orange cover the cold ground. The Seagull arrives home to find his wife—my avocado-loving ex-fiancée—sitting on a rocking chair breastfeeding their child in the mid-afternoon, the daylight waning in the room. The Seagull walks across the cabin and greets them, kisses his wife on the forehead, then smiles as the baby boy's small fist opens and closes as he feeds.

"I saw him today," The Seagull says to her.

His wife offers the baby her other breast. "How did he look?"

"Exhausted. He's trying to finish his book."

"You're good to him," his wife says and smiles. "You're good to his characters, too."

The Seagull does a lazy spin-kick. "They need me," he says, taking his inky black hair out of the tight ponytail and letting it fall across his shoulder blades, his bald dome gleaming in the cabin's last gasps of light. He then rubs his child's bald dome. "Someday they'll need him, too," The Seagull says.

And there they stay, this enchanted family, the champions of the lonely and the broken, the people aching to look at another person and say, "Namaste." Someday it could be you on the verge of some vertiginous crisis, tip-toeing a line that's barely drawn; someday maybe you'll answer the door, or look up from an elliptical machine's dashboard, or maybe you'll gaze out the window and spot a guy with a bald dome and inky black hair pulled into a tight ponytail, his billowy white wings sprouting from his shoulder blades.

Or maybe, someday in the not-too distant future, it will be The Son of The Seagull, performing his father's poetry and martial arts and miracles, a celestial child that the future will also long to know.

The Day I Went to See Steven Seagal

I was tired of trying to finish this book. I'd spent most of my time avoiding my writing space—an old plywood desk and a chair I bought at a yard sale, an old laptop and a gooseneck lamp.

One night, I turned off all the lights in my apartment and danced in the dark while listening to Bruce Springsteen's "Dancing in the Dark." The song spoke to me, and I hop-stepped while swinging my arms and snapping my fingers. In the dark. When I was tired of dancing, I went to bed without writing a word.

The next morning, I scrambled some eggs and cooked crisp bacon and read the free weekly delivered to my apartment. One of articles said that Steven Seagal was shooting a movie in downtown Northboro and the filmmakers were looking for extras. I could either finish this book, or venture downtown and land a gig as an extra in a Steven Seagal movie.

It was a simple decision.

A portion of downtown Northboro was blocked off with yellow police tape, and I told the Uber driver, whose name was Dennis and looked vaguely familiar, to drop me off at a gas station and I'd walk the rest. "Good luck with the ending, Nate," the driver said.

"What are you talking about?" I asked and ducked under the yellow tape and roamed the streets where there were trailers and cameras and racks of lights on rollers.

I turned into a bar where a forty-something guy and a blonde girl with a scar above her top lip were passing a bowl. The girl waved at me. "Hi Nate," she said with a slight lisp. "How's the book coming?"

"Do I know you?" I asked her.

"Nate is a riot, Rocco," she said and turned to the guy who was tall and handsome and wore a Red Sox hat with the brim broken in. Upon closer inspection, he looked familiar, too. They both did.

"He is a riot," the man said.

"Are you being flippant?" the girl asked him, cocking her hip and winking at him. "Don't make me punish you."

"I'm married, Texas," Rocco said, handing her the glass-blown bowl and turning to me. "How's the book coming, Nate?"

"How did you know I'm writing a book?" I asked.

Rocco laughed. "You're a riot, buddy. Good luck with the ending."

I walked into the bar, which had a wooden interior and an Old Western-motif, a player piano in the corner and sawdust on the floors. There was a poker game at a table by the entrance, the men holding their cards close to their faces while smoking cigars. The bar was packed, most people congregating in a back room that was entered through swinging saloon doors. Again, all of the people at the bar seemed familiar. A neck-less man with biceps the size of bowling balls cranked out one-armed push-ups on the floor next to the only open stool. "You can have that seat, Nate," the man said between reps. "I'm about to head home to my baby girl."

"How do you know my name?"

The man stopped in a plank pose and grinned. "You're a riot, Nate," he said. "When are you going to finish your book?"

Then it hit me. "Holy shit, Sean! I thought I made you disappear!"

"That was just a story, Nate."

Indeed, these were all if my characters assembled in the same bar in downtown Northboro. There, at the end, Aleister Bowman sipped a martini in a tweed coat and a sheer white scarf while chatting up the poet James C. Hoffman. With Nugget perched on her shoulder, Priscilla sat in a booth between Jed and Willy, splitting a pitcher of beer as Priscilla's son Donald sulked beside them.

"What's going on in back?" I asked Sean while he busted out more push-ups.

"Steven Seagal is here," Sean said, the veins bulging from his neck. "Your whole book has been building up to this scene."

"How do you know that? You're just a character," I said.

"You're a riot, Nate."

I worked my way through the crowd of my characters and entered the back room through the swinging saloon doors. The Andre Whittaker Trio was playing soft jazz in the back corner. The Northboro High School Class of 1993 line-danced in front of them. Al, wearing a pacemaker, and Seth with a new full head of hair were engaged a good old-fashioned arm-wrestling match.

And there, holding court at a table with Eloise in her daughter's slinky blue dress and Jocelyn with the white bow in her hair and Tiffany in her yoga clothes sat the inimitable Steven Seagal. Squat and pudgier than I anticipated, Steven Seagal had a bald dome and inky black hair pulled into a tight ponytail. He was sipping vodka from a highball glass and smiled at me as I approached the table.

He stood up to shake my hand. "Nate, we meet again. I've been waiting the whole book for this moment."

"You're not Steven Seagal," I said.

"This is the ending, Nate," The Seagull said.

"I've been waiting for this," I said.

"You always knew," The Seagull said and pressed his palms together in front of his heart, bowing his head. "Namaste, Nate."

"Namaste, Seagull."

Then he stood and lifted me into his arms as billowy white wings sprouted from his shoulder blades. He carried me through the saloon doors and out the entrance to the bar. Once outside, we ascended toward the clouds. And we flew into a pink sky as the sun set on the horizon, and I knew this was it. This was how it ends—with me being saved, my faith restored.

Nathan Graziano lives in Manchester, New Hampshire, with his wife and kids. His books include *Teaching Metaphors* (Sunnyoutside Press), *After the Honeymoon* (Sunnyoutside Press) *Hangover Breakfasts* (Bottle of Smoke Press in 2012), *Sort Some Sort of Ugly* (Marginalia Publishing in 2013), and *My Next Bad Decision* (Artistically Declined Press, 2014). *Almost Christmas*, a collection of short prose pieces, was published by Redneck Press in 2017. For more information, visit his website: www.nathangraziano.com.